MISSING MARGATE

MISSING MARGATE

Michael Bracewell

Fourth Estate · London

First Published in Great Britain by
Fourth Estate Limited
113 Westbourne Grove
London W2 4UP

Copyright © 1988 by Michael Bracewell

British Library Cataloguing in Publication Data
Bracewell, Michael *1958–*
Missing Margate
I.   Title
823'.914 [F]

ISBN 1-872180-71-X

Typeset by York House Typographic Ltd, London W7
Printed by Richard Clay Ltd, Bungay

For Michael Woods and Susan Martin

Contents

Andy – I am not here anymore but I am fine.

Love, Billy

(Farewell note to Andy Warhol from Billy Name)

Beside the Queen's Highcliffe now rank grows the vetch,
Now dark is the terrace, a storm-battered stretch;
And I think, as the fairy-lit sights I recall,
It is those we are fighting for, foremost of all.
(Sir John Betjeman, 'Margate 1940')

MISSING MARGATE

Introduction

As one New York analyst wrote recently apropos this new frenzied consumer conciousness, there is now a 'new type of patient' who is presenting himself. The classical neurotic for whom psychoanalysis was invented suffered from symptoms which were lodged in a self that was otherwise intact. By contrast, the 'new patient' of the post-modern period has not even progressed to the point where a stable identity structure has coalesced. 'Typically he or she suffers from feelings of emptiness, isolation and futility, pre-Oedipal rage and primitive separation . . . which are masked by grandiose narcissistic fantasies', fuelled by 'the marked intensification of the pursuit of material success, power and status; an increased preoccupation with youth, health and glamour, accompanied by difficulty in forming relationships with emotional depth.' Excessive alienated narcissism frequently masked by social adaptability has come to dominate our era, according to this perception, just as hysteria and (later) neurosis did Freud's.

(Brandon Taylor, 'After Post-Modernism', with reference to J. Whitebrook, 'Reason and Happiness: Some Psychoanalytic Themes in Critical Theory', in R. J. Bernstein (ed), 'Habermas and Modernity', 1985, p. 150.)

1

THE HESITATION OF
EMPEDOCLES

One: No One Knows Your Name

THE BLEACHED pavement rose up to Max de Winter's undefended eyes as he stumbled out of Duchess Street W1 and then stopped, wavering a little despite its solidity because Max wasn't feeling very well. On the freshly scrubbed façade of the BBC building that Max proceeded to lean spitting and cursing against, red-faced and breathless, the slogan

NATION SHALL SPEAK PEACE UNTO NATION

seemed – despite the authority of its sans-serif, no-nonsense capitals – somehow inappropriate.

The early-afternoon sun made Max's eyes ache terribly,

and he squinted nastily at a passing Arts Administrator before wiping some excess saliva from the corner of his mouth with the back of his hand. He had left his sunglasses on a bistro table in New Cavendish Street, and was predicting their subsequent theft and destruction at the hands of the professionally rude waiter. His thought patterns were laced with the tearfully self-righteous suspicion and oath-laden outrage that frequently attach themselves to a self-pitying, physically uncertain and hopelessly drunk young man. The sunglasses were important to Max, his only mask to advance behind, and life seemed unbearable without them.

As he swayed like a tall building in the slipstream of Hurricane Rayban the glasses took on a totemistic significance, and their loss seemed to verify that in some underhand, insidious kind of way his right to have any say at all in his destiny had been taken away from him.

Max clasped the sides of his head and moaned quietly, his extravagant emotion giving rise to much twitching of net curtains in the windows of the office across the street which had been cunningly degentrified to make it look like an office.

The traffic moved on across the lights and Max crouched sobbing on the pavement, his hunched and defeated aspect being gradually obscured by a mist of russet exhaust. It was, one could say, operatic.

It was also the day of The Big Launch, and the atmosphere around Fitzrovia, along Cleveland Street, along Goodge and Mortimer Streets, gusting beside the Diuretic Unit of Middlesex Hospital, sneaking down Tottenham

Mews and emerging with a self-conscious flourish – 'There!' – into the electronics retail end of Tottenham Court Road had driven this section of West One quite rigid with indifference.

It was the day of the Big Launch of *Designate* magazine: a new and exciting look at the future style of tomorrow yesterday – or today, or next week. Last year, possibly – the definition is irrelevant; the point of the thing is style, and *Designate* magazine had wide enough margins to make anything stylish.

Max de Winter walked into one of the elegant pillars which support the soaring needle spire of All Souls and was by that time past caring whether the future was here today or gone the day before. His past and his future no longer seemed to meet in his present and the style of this confusion was of little interest to him. He wasn't there. Not really.

Max de Winter wasn't there either when Malcolm Houston, the new and exciting editor of *Designate*, was addressing his staff with the same mixture of generosity and weariness with which one addresses Christmas cards on the subject of young blood, old wood and fresh pastures.

This was at the big planning meeting. A room had been appointed with a view of the car park of the neighbouring television headquarters, and coffee was poured from a triangular stainless steel coffee pot with a parrot-yellow handle and a spout the hue of July blue. As the coffee was drunk – ritualistically, one might say – the clever triangular beakers were scattered with precision among dunes of forward profiling sheets, advertising copy and provocatively opened diaries.

Rough sketches were made in moments of wild inspiration on the backs of proof sheets, and the illegible crudity of these illustrations remained in the centre of the table as evidence of their intention to attract favour from the editor as opposed to demonstrate a point. Black fibre-tip pens were sucked and fiddled with. Telephone numbers were seized with religious fervour out of the heated wardrobes of fame-hungry brains, and repeated litany-like by their captor until noted down as 'interesting'.

It was feeding time at the latest glossy.

Malcolm was very frank about the cut of his jib, the tightness of his ship and the passenger-hostile persuasion that he expected of his crew. Heads nodded fervently at the mention of 'commitment', and watery smiles swam magically across tense faces when evening and weekend input was stressed. Knuckles crackled with the urge to impress and not one knuckle crackled more urgently than those belonging to Arabella Cloth, the exciting new Assistant Editor (Features) who sat on Malcolm's left.

Sitting on Malcolm's left was a way of not looking at Malcolm, and thus subordination could coexist with Individual Flair by virtue of the lack of eye contact. Arabella looked hard at the table top and nodded when Malcolm outlined the market gap that *Designate* hoped to fill. She shook her head when Malcolm suggested (by way of proving himself open to criticism) that they might have made some errors in their brand-profiling age-groupwise. It was vital to commence both the venture and the planning meeting with a ritual of self-questioning. The admission of possible error (although not for one moment believed) served a vital role in establishing a backdrop of bogus maturity and clear-headedness against which the team could then act out their wildest schemes without fear of seeming any less than professional.

An oriental dissonance filled the air when Malcolm said 'Are we ready to go for this one? If we're not – we should say so.' And it was at this point that Arabella shook her head. She just shook her head without moving her lips or looking at anybody. She shook her henna'd ringlets and Soviet ceramic ear-rings by way of a token genuflection to ward off the evil spirits of Marketing Doubt and Product Insecurity, those gremlins within the periodical publishing machine. She was silently saying (as she shook her head), 'No Malcolm – we will not let you down. We are ready to go for this one.' Arabella was itching to shine and knew that one moment's misplaced visible or vocal enthusiasm could eclipse her rising star with its cloud of unprofessional effervescence.

Max de Winter was lying on his back in the Chelsea Physic Garden when Gemma Danvers (Deputy Editor 'In and Out' section and Advertising) choked on a piece of chewing gum whilst trying to make herself heard during the debate on a projected feature entitled 'New City Men: Who Are They?'

Max de Winter was inhaling verbena by the stone lip of a fountain and thinking how, given just a little strength, he would simply press a button and disappear whilst the

Designate team turned their media-sodden gaze to him and decided that he would make a splendid feature.

Knowing his little army to march on sycophancy as well as fear, Malcolm had shared a joke with the troops in order to win their support for this his best (and only) idea for an in-depth *Designate* styled feature.

'You know when Bill Wilson over at Channel 8 – the new late-late independent cable – ah, told me about their profiling of Max de Winter Associates, I have to tell you I thought he was crazy. And I'm telling you that. I thought he was crazy. I said "Bill, you must be out of your mind. De Winter is just – not – fucking – famous enough."' (laughter). ' "He's not even a potential revival." ' (Hysterical laughter, the team are in stitches. Gemma used the general moment of shared hilarity as a cover for pouring herself another cup of coffee out of the terrifyingly awkward-to-lift coffee pot which was just out of reach; others lit cigarettes as they laughed – all these actions thus doubling as guarantees that the laughter was quite genuine and uncontrollable because it continued even as they did other things. It was therefore a moment of regrouping and rearming disguised as applause for Malcolm's anecdote.)

And now it must be said that Max de Winter and Max de Winter Associates were names to respect, for the very same Max de Winter whom we discovered unwell at the junction of Duchess Street and Portland Place (and who subsequently has been observed inhaling soft scent in the Chelsea Physic Garden) is the most brilliant young architect in England – he who shaped the new London skyline into an aphorism that summed up the age in architectural language and then under-lined it with glorious style by marrying the beautiful Rebecca Walters, erstwhile child-neurotic turned Cork Street Fine Art dealer *par excellence* whose glamorous gallery is the International launch pad of the effortlessly uncommercial.

Malcolm looked around the table for a minute and then continued: 'So then I got to thinking – and I'm telling you this now – then I got to thinking, "Well, it's a strange world, and maybe there's a story in this architect after all."' He leaned forward slightly, a man just testing ideas, a man just – running a few things up the flagpole to see if anyone salutes.

'De Winter is just turned thirty. He's responsible for some of the most controversial office buildings in the City. London Wall will never be the same – but he's a bit of a mystery. So I think, mystery – Howard Hughes – gothic – meetings in car parks – sudden departures from restaurants – receiving the Hands On Design Award *in absentia* – a place out of town. He's so public . . . '

'Yet so private?' suggested Gemma, hopefully.

'Possibly, Gemma, possibly. But what I was thinking of was this: we do a feature on de Winter buildings and stress the anonymity of their architect by implication. We stress the 'Corporate Structuring: What Is It?' angle. We do a late-seventies Fritz Laing/Art School throwback, but new. I want the visuals to say 'Desire' and I want them to say 'Power' – the romance of the post-bang Career/Aesthetics interface when investment consultants have that kind of David Bowie, photochromatic-glasses, glamour. I want to make Eurobond dealers screen-dump finance projections in a way that would look good in *Designate*. The de Winter buildings are a feature of New City Youth – pan-financial, slick, colourful – a little sinister. So what's the guy like who built them? What does he wear? How's his marriage? What's his aftershave? What's his opinion on religion? Does he eat out a lot? I'm putting you on this one Arabella, issue five, the *Designate* Finance Supplement.

Max de Winter was lying in the long grass of a small London garden when *Designate* decided to feature him. It was an evening in June, threatening thunder above the dulled roar of the traffic, and sentimentalists would have noted the brevity of the lilac that year. He watched the evening airliners glinting in the sun, their silver underbellies shining like magnesium fish drifting through tinted water. He kept falling asleep. In the middle distance, across the river from Chelsea – the conservatory of London – some youths were vandalising the peace temple. Max wrote letters to himself in his head.

'If I were to see the components of my life from without, would I envy the owner who is by titular right alone myself?'

And the tone of his questions reminded him of the ludicrous and stupid rantings to be found in the London evening papers.

'Why, oh why, oh why . . . I, for one . . . '

He felt drowsy. 'I never share anything, and thus I never possess or colonise anything – I don't own anything. I am a vagrant, a venture vagrant. I should have got into property, not designed it. I can't stand this dot matrix of bits of a life that I wander around, unable to stand back and see the picture, or self-portrait, that their combined number – hopefully – creates.'

And then he fell asleep, vivid and various dreams stealing out of the shrubs and flowering alpines of Chelsea to torment him with their fidelity to the real-life originators of their teasing characters. He kept seeing his beautiful wife Rebecca, only as she was once, not as she was now, and then seeing the garden at New Manderley, their place in the country.

In Max de Winter's dream, lunch had raised Rebecca and him above the animals. For the first, second or last time, he was standing on the steps of St Paul's listening to the sound of a wasp trapped behind the blinds of a summer's morning. There was also a waltz-time in progress, wafting on baked breeze from the Croissant Express in Leadenhall Market. With rings on her fingers and bells on her toes the bells of St Paul's chimed out across the city whilst Max de Winter waited for his wife.

For the first, second or third Mrs de Winter. Max had only married once but been separated three times and reunited twice. Away from Rebecca his work suffered and his physical condition grew steadily worse, but married or separated they loved one another and that was the basis of the problem.

Max dreamt of the rain pouring over the fields and black leaves gusting across the stubble, a heavy scent coming off the greasy shoots and damp earth. A whisper of autumn in spring.

And then there was Rebecca, who had returned to him Persephone-like last spring and then gone away again whilst he was designing the Historic Invoices Library for the Museum of Corporate Finance. He had waited for her to come back to him again, this spring, and she hadn't, so he just kind of waited around, scratching his ear from time to time and staring moodily into shop windows in St Christopher's Place. When she was last with him she had seemed different; those loved features had changed and she was no longer the glamorous blend of despot and doll, suffragette and usherette that had confused the gossip columnists of three continents. And he, Max de Winter, the most celebrated young architect in England! Was nothing good enough?

But lying on his back in the grass, now that he could no longer feel anything, and now that he'd more or less given up being an architect, now – now it was difficult to imagine a better evening for giving up everything, the weather being ideal.

In his dream he was standing on the Whispering Gallery of St Paul's. He looked like Leslie Howard. He was wearing a raincoat and smoking a pipe, leaning forward slightly to smile in a fatherly way at four Tommies. It was the Second World War . . .

Max was never really sure where the four Tommies had originally come from, but he was always pleased to see them. AWOL, lost, or legitimately Doing The Town, these four cheery privates would materialise in Max's mind with all the ruddy vigour and down-to-earth decency that one would expect from a quartet of the nation's finest. It was his relationship with them that was . . . odd. Rebecca used to comment on it. 'Max!' she would whisper urgently looking into his eyes for a glimmer of recognition, 'Max! Darling! What do you see? Is it the squaddies again? Tell me – it's Rebecca darling, your wife . . . ' And then she would shake him by the wrists, several minutes generally passing until he slowly turned his head to her with curious robotic jerks to look at her in total bewilderment before coming to. As his marriage failed and his hatred of his career increased he saw more and more of these sons of Britain for whom the empire was a sunnier, more purposeful place.

When Max dreamt of St Paul's, and when he encountered the Tommies upon it or within it, he was filled with a new energy that communicated itself as a faith in something. He took on the facial expression of Leslie Howard, and his hock-spritzèr-stained architect's raincoat became a goodly pristine weather-proof. His eyes twinkled with knowing patriotism as he turned against the wind to light his pipe, and England, his England, became a place totally unlike the one his conscious hours of existence were troubled by.

The first time he met the Tommies they were all Lending A Hand in the making of a short film. Max joined in. The enthusiastic young man from Cambridge who had worked for the Varsity film unit before the war was only too pleased to work with 'real chaps'.

'This is even better than Mass Observation!' he chortled, busily arranging his little crew into a prototype of the documentary goon-squads who would race round the capital on the amphetamine of pure self-importance some fifty years later. Together Max and the Tommies made a twenty-minute propaganda film. It was called 'Going Our Way?' and involved much use of the thumbs-up salute on the part of the Tommies and even more cheerful discussion on the part of Max about the notion of Commonwealth democracy that was being defended by Those Who Served. It was a very worthwhile film.

The trouble was that Max never knew what drew him into the period and company of the Tommies. Was it a longing for something to fight for and believe in? Was it simply that he needed friends and found his own age surprisingly hostile? Or was it some deep-rooted and outraged sense of patriotism that found solace only within a subconscious recreation of the Blitz Spirit? All of these options were unlikely. St Paul's, the Battle of Britain, the Tommies – all of these archaic phenomena were nothing more than the point at which the strands of Max's neurosis met. They were the point of visualisation. It could have been anything – a department store or spring on the Rive Gauche, any mental landscape that took over when anxiety reached overload. As it was it was the Tommies, and they were a decent enough bunch of blokes. Max knew he would never really go their way, but the pretence of beginning a journey with them afforded him some kind of exhausted comfort before his everyday self crawled wearily back into the jostling nervousness of reality.

When awake, Max de Winter had been feeling tired for nearly fourteen months. It was always important to him to be somewhere else, to be somewhere different from wherever he happened to be. This involved a lot of travel. He was always trying to find The Other Place, and never could. He ran out of conferences on Brushed Aluminium and Decorative Lagging at the Building Design Centre, desperate for some Cool Alley by the river or a cemetery near Leicester. He would arrive at his office in the mid-morning and bark suggestions to his incredulous staff with a crazed enthusiasm that utterly belied the fact that by lunch time he would have gone away again, his mind a stroboscopic chamber of meaningless images, each one hinged to its neighbour with the touch-welding adhesive of liquid panic that was secreted daily out of his crushed subconscious.

Even as the *Designate* profile research team were thumbing through the Royal Institute of British Architects Directory in search of a contact number for their prey, the subject of their research was stumbling around London in an ankle-length raincoat and increasingly dusty suit. Added to this organic vagrancy was a new pair of sun-glasses – tortoiseshell frames and gold rims, the lenses a stagnant mill-pond green.

Back at *Designate* the interview sheet was being drawn up amidst much 'Oh yes, that would be interesting' and 'Let's save that one.'

'What does success mean to you?'

'Are you interested in designing for the Chicago Art Fair as rumoured in *The Urbanist*?'

'How do Rebecca and yourself relax?'

'What advice would you give to a young architect?'

But Max de Winter had just one question, and this he addressed to himself all the time:

'How do I stop being Max de Winter?'

His dreams were moulded to the venue and circumstances of the cerebral pot-holing that he was forced to call sleep, but more and more frequently, dreaming whilst awake, he reinvented himself as a traditionalist, an Englishman, and a professional – one of those whose efforts were now paying back their toil with an insight into the philosophy of the Greater Game.

But what was the Greater Game? It should not, he reasoned, be a sport played simply for the sake of winning. Only the vulgar young lions for whom success was a matter of competitive remuneration played merely to win. Max de Winter despised the new City citizens who danced upon the grave of reason in celebration of the redundancy of the Eternal Horologist who had tended to his cogs and chains with something more than the liquid grease of textbook executive management.

Even as Max sank deeper and deeper into despair he knew that it was those sycophants to fashionable business sophistry who had the ownership of tomorrow. Tomorrow most probably belonged to them by virtue of a shrewd down payment the previous fiscal.

Oh yes, they knew the ropes, they knew their way around. Buy in Hackney before it goes through the roof! Too late! Buy in Oval whilst it's still stable. Too late again! Ever thought of the Home Counties? Henley, perhaps, or the nice bit of St Albans? Anticipate the spread of the commuter belt, wait for the waist-line of London to bulge out a little more in the direction of cheaper property. Wait for it, then wait for it, then – Coronary Now! Big Bang! A nation of shopkeepers and stylists. Then take advantage of the convalescence of the heart, watch it growing stronger daily in your little bit of England. Never mind the flutter, go for serious speculations, and then relax, in the Fulham Palace Road, with clever rustic cooking from somewhere your grandmother had never heard of and a bit of pompous chat about tax shelters and the market. Be smart, get with it – think of the Pecking Order and the Company Ladder.

And this was when Max de Winter saw well dressed corpses in rusting company Saabs as he sketched in obsessive Rotring on thin architectural paper the Mahlerian moods of his nightmare corporations.

In his dreams Max knew an older England. The pictures of faded postcards brought tears to his eyes as he travelled up and down in the lift in Heal's. He was permitted this eccentricity by the prerogative due to a shopper's account holder and the ownership of a gold charge card. Occasionally he would get out and buy something – a carpet perhaps, or a dinner service. These would be sent down to New Manderley on the instruction of the cheerful assistant from Highgate and then Max would haughtily return to his lift, disappearing upwards or downwards depending on which way the lift arrived. This would go on for maybe two hours.

Unshaven, his dull eyes hidden behind green glasses, Max spent his days on the move because to stop was to sleep was to dream.

St Paul's, June 1940, the azure above Wren's dome a wreath of dogfight curls. The four Tommies were always there at the start of the dream. Sometmes they were journalists dressed as Tommies and other times they were Building Fabric representatives. Max told them why they were Dying for Their Country and they were respectfully grateful for having had their fate explained to them by a gentleman.

He would point from the dome of St Paul's in the direction of Stratford-upon-Avon and then muse reverently about Shakespeare for the Tommies' general good. He told them about their history, about Raleigh and Pitt, Wellington and Robin Hood. He was really talking to them about Rebecca, only he couldn't bring himself to say her name.

In his sleep this all made perfect sense, but the glue of dreams makes flypapers of us all and in the slightest breeze we tangle. Max de Winter, a projected feature in exciting new *Designate* magazine, was knotting in the wind.

Whether Max de Winter's dreams were the result of continued inhalation of the potent ozone of pure self-criticism was not a Problem To Be Solved noted in grey fibre-tip on the 24 June a.m. page of Arabella Cloth's Personal Organiser as she walked briskly down Oxford Street from Marble Arch en route to her working breakfast in Soho.

Arabella loved getting up and going to work. Most of all she loved ringing people up before she left her flat to tell them how busy she was. This happy generalisation, when underlined by the all-important Deadline of a working breakfast, was all that Arabella needed to put on for the day by way of accessory to her armour-like uniform of black clothing.

The morning was cool and overcast, Oxford Street not yet a cattle drive. Here and there a chemist was open, and postcard racks of happy topless girls and florid pop stars stood rakishly outside on the pavement, chained to the wall.

Arabella made a mental note to write a small item for the 'In and Out' section of *Designate* about the colonisation of West One by the working population of the outer suburbs. Oxford Street was, after all, the High Street of England, indistinguishable in its cast of shops from Norwich, say, or even Croydon. This was the worn out oesophagus of London, where massive mouthfuls of money were lubricated by the saliva of retail design in order to slip effortlessly into the stomach of business. The money was then broken down by all the little enzymes employed by business corporations to keep the process working. Shopping in Oxford Street is the only organic junk food to satisfy the massive hunger of England for a healthy diet.

This, however, was not a process that people like Arabella had to participate in. Arabella was clothed and shod on a strictly one-to-one basis.

She turned down Argyll Street, where the slower air smelt of stale fruit, and allowed herself a sideways glance into one of the smaller shops. This was research, not window shopping. Then she paused at the newspaper stand opposite Liberty's to buy *Business* and *Ceramics* and noted with pride that *Designate* had nearly sold out. She had reached that peak of achievement in magazine buying as art form and compulsory professional skill where hunting for change in her rubber purse actually cheered the news-vendor up, so elegant and articulate was it in uniting the designer of the periodical machine with its mechanic's oily rag. The news-vendor waited respectfully for the inevitable twenty-pound note with the cheerful patience of an old and trusted family servant, his print-darkened fingers flexing with an eagerness to please in the depths of his change apron. Arabella would use the useful tenner and brace of pound coins that she received back from him to pay for her breakfast (reclaimable) and a taxi back to the office.

Past poor Shelley's house in Poland Street and so into Soho, the cosmetically embalmed corpse of sleaze where builders' skips are both the cross on the door and the tombstone of those fittings. Soho, the graveyard of frolic. Busy ghosts flitted across the set of this depressing musical, film directors all, and longing to be the subject of their own documentaries. If Arabella's business ego were to grow any larger as the result of her working breakfast in Soho it would have to apply for planning permission.

Morning spread over London like a broken egg, and some, like Max de Winter, were drowning in the yolk. Arabella turned into Old Compton Street and bought some more magazines for the hell of it so that by the time she reached her favourite patisserie where the working breakfast was scheduled to take place the black leather strap of her black leather rucksack was biting into her white shoulder and sending shivers all the way down to her black heart.

Max de Winter was colouring in the Arts page of his morning paper. He too was on his way to work, but there was little point in it. His studio was based on the edge of the City, the semimirrored glazing of its windows hanging like plastic raindrops in the fringe of London Wall. Max de Winter will never design another building. He can no longer see the structures in his mind or visualise their components. He can no longer envisage the frame, the omniplatz, the lift shafts, the cooling ducts, the mezzanine cloakroom or the subterranean squash court. He used to be able to visit these places in his mind, transcribing his patrols onto drawing paper. Now he can't. He can no longer see anything, or look forward to anything. His imagination puts all energy into his dreams.

There is one early-morning dream which he sees in the mirror of his office washroom. In it the brief midwinter twilight hangs low over Bankside and nobody will ever tell a joke again. The Battle of Britain is over, and the Tommies are all dead. They never lived to hear about George Baselitz, the Café Pelican, or the Pet Shop Boys. Times have changed, and there are different needs. Max dreamt that after the death of the Tommies another battle began, The Battle of London, and this was the one in which Max de Winter attacked the Capital. As yet there was merely an abrogation of the uneasy peace treaty that existed between Max and the City, and the air around

Charter Lane was heavy with cordite, the stench of guns that had merely cleared their throats in polite anticipation of a war.

Arabella, unaware of these hostilities, ordered hot chocolate and counted her magazines. This passed the time until Paul Vince, the Press Officer to Max de Winter Associates, arrived with a slightly chiselled look in his eyes to explain to Arabella that Max de Winter would not be available for interview in *Designate*.

'Of course de Winter Associates is swiftly becoming one of the leading corporate business building practices in the UK,' he whispered, 'and of course Max himself has become one of the leading lights of the architectural scene and something of a celebrity . . . ' A shower of brochures and press releases were offered to the professionally disappointed but personally relieved Arabella.

'All his main buildings are described in these – D'Arblays Trust, Pacman Software, the Self & Assurance . . . Ah, here's one you might find interesting for your magazine, Max de Winter's unique design for the Church of God the Truth in Tower Hill. Oddball sect but a brilliant use of slate.'

Arabella looked carefully at the brochures, inwardly calculating how long she ought to look at each one in order to give the impression that she was reading the complex columns of building data as opposed to simply looking at the dramatic pictures.

'But we are very keen to talk to Max,' she said. 'I was rather hoping we could set up a meeting.'

Paul Vince tensed.

'He's extremely busy right now; the Historic Invoices Library is really taking up time and of course it's July soon . . .'

'July?'

'The Urban Ergonomics conference in Sâo Paulo. Max will be speaking, of course, unless the Paris Community Housing seminar is set back yet again – you know how it is.'

'We'd only want him for an afternoon – for lunch?'

'I'm sorry. Max did ask me to tell you that he will be most happy to give you access to drawings, architectural models, etcetera, but an interview – so sorry.'

Somewhere in the back of her mind Arabella could see greedy black vultures circling over the dying body of her first *Designate* profile feature. She began to worry.

'Could we talk to Rebecca? Is she still in Cork Street?'

'She was the last time we heard. They're separated, you know.'

'Again?' squeaked Arabella.

Paul looked at the table cloth and nodded sadly.

'Is that why Max won't be interviewed – depression?'

'I'd leave the dirt to the dailies,' said Paul. 'And now I must dash. It's the same again at Channel 8 in twenty minutes and I can't spend too long on each refusal. Nice to have met you, anyway.' And then he was gone.

Arabella wondered whether it was worth pretending to resign in order to prove her commitment in the wake of her failure. She decided it wasn't, but felt almost interested in Max de Winter.

The Friday when Arabella had her working breakfast with Paul Vince was the tense last act of an anxious week for Max de Winter. As he waited for Vince to report back to him he stood with his face pressed against the window of his office and thought about the garden at New Manderley. At New Manderley, in the evening, you could hear the peacocks scream and watch the somnambulistic progress of a pollen-gorged bee as it hovered round a flower. In the twilight you could sometimes see a peacock perching high on the ancient wall that surrounded the garden, its black eyes fixed on the reddening sky.

All of Max de Winter's buildings in London, the five that crowned his success, seemed to be forming a circle around him in the hope of discovering a truth. They were like inquisitive journalists, and there was shoving at the back. Max de Winter did not want anyone to know his name. He didn't want to leave anything behind him after he'd gone. It was as simple as that.

Paul Vince was soon back in the office, and Max turned slowly to look at him.

'Well?'

'I don't think they're going to follow up,' said Paul. 'They're looking for stylists, figureheads of the New London. The usual lifestyle design commentary thing.'

'I see,' said Max, playing with the tungsten stapler, 'they want to know whether I'm excited or busy, and then take a photograph of me in a room with a charcoal carpet.'

'That kind of thing,' agreed Vince.

'Well, my head will never be on their pike, never, ever.'

Paul Vince sat down and opened his mouth, a little speech preparing itself in his mind.

Max continued, 'Why do people make chairs out of old motorbikes?' he asked, interview style.

'Image profile?' suggested Paul, brightly.

'I don't think so,' murmured Max.

A dark-grey moment wandered slowly across the room like a well bred secretary looking for a biro.

'Are there any imminent commissions?' asked Max. 'Or bad debts, or lawsuits, or press conferences?'

'You're all clear,' replied Paul. 'The Invoices Library is in fact ahead of schedule except for the Swedes and their energy-saving ionisers that are causing the boys in Finishing a bit of a headache, but other than that' (he checked his notes) . . . 'It's seminar time, Paris, São Paulo, and Herr Greutchen faxed in a positive structuring leaflet from Düsseldorf – he wants you to talk about the omniplatz at Pacman Software.'

Max groaned. 'Why?'

Paul checked his notes again. 'It's . . . radical.'

'It's frightening,' said Max. 'Four thousand square feet of compressed rubber holding down a triple layer of service ducts. If a pipe bursts the thing'll go off like a bomb.' He was quiet for a moment. 'Imagine . . . '

Paul looked back at his notes. 'Our client response questionnaire found that 78 per cent of the Pacman workforce found the building a major contribution to de-stress. The 28 per cent of those who are also at manage-ment or executive level reported that absenteeism due to boredom-spiral has dropped significantly.' He paused. 'But they don't like the colour.'

'It's white,' said Max.

Paul checked his notes again. 'Surgical, hostile . . . effeminate, cold, hot, boring, alien, too bright, pretentious . . . unprofessional . . . '

'And Spain,' said Max, 'is so cheap once you've got there.'

Paul blinked and looked at the laces of his shoes. He put the Pacman file down very carefully and then drew a deep breath. 'Max,' he announced, 'I've known you for a long time now and I think I can say that in those four months I've never seen you as in need of a long holiday as you are now.'

'Thank you, Paul. Go away.'

Paul stood up, pretending to want to argue. It was Friday, the day of the long lunches, so he left the room anyway.

And then Max was alone.

As Max de Winter left the office by a side exit, a rhomboid of yellow sunlight fell sharply across his back and followed him down the metal staircase. Max knew he would never return to the office, so he left the side door open.

The dusk of his Badoit and Babycham days had surely come. He had only to count the thousand silver milk churns in which he was storing for some inexplicable purpose the gallons of tears and spilt milk that he had accumulated during his career and his marriage.

Pacman Software, D'Arblays, Self & Assurance, The

Historic Invoices Library of the Museum of Corporate Finance, and the Church of God the Truth, Tower Hill. Those were his five greatest buildings, and they were all in the City of London. Those were the things that he loved and must kill.

Walking up Fish Street in the sun, he could see the scarlet wigwam water tank that stood high on the roof of his Self & Assurance building. It was maybe two streets away. He made his way down a dark alley and came out into a dazzling white piazza. There was nobody around and the breeze brought the sound of a distant rustling, the litter of a thousand sandwich lunches, the thought of all those paper bags. Max stood in front of the twenty storeys of blue glass that were the Self & Assurance London headquarters.

'Movement 5', a work in steel salvaged from the debris of the building that used to occupy the piazza, stood forlornly on a little concrete plinth to Max's right. It cast a jagged shadow in the murk of which a lolly stick could be seen.

Max ran his finger sadly across the brass plate that was fastened to the wall of Self & Assurance in a little mock-classical alcove. 'Max de Winter Associates 1986' it read.

Rubbing the 6 thoughtfully, Max formed some words in his head. The plan he decided upon can be articulated as follows:

'As the architect of this building and its four brothers in the neighbourhood I reclaim the right to destroy my own work. I do not suppose this right exists but I reclaim it nonetheless. I hereby exchange the theodolite for dynamite and the slide rule for a bomb. I will take out all five of the buildings that I have designed. There will be nothing left. These buildings were my signature, my name on the horizon, and I shall cross them out. I want to know that no one knows my name. Maybe no one does. Rebecca does – in the sunny corridors of her complex – but she always was an obsessive note taker. However, I want nothing but rubble, no sense, no meaning, and no name.'

As he left the Self & Assurance piazza he remembered his very first commission. Not so much a house as a hacienda, in Margate. It had paid for the wheels on his E-Type, that hacienda in Margate. He would commit no acts of terrorism in Margate.

'He's called Max de Winter,' said Arabella with growing impatience as she hurried along to Malcolm Houston's office with little time to waste on the slow-witted Gemma Danvers who trotted along beside her, pearls bouncing about the lace collar of her blouse, 'and he won't give us an interview. Malcolm will be furious.' Gemma agreed that he probably would be.

But Malcolm was strangely calm as Arabella sat in one of his low office chairs with her face a mask of total commitment and mature responsibility.

'Call up Rupert Goodwyn for the photographs,' said Malcolm. 'He's very exciting. And then have a meeting with Betty about the fashion coverage and blend the two. I know that Betty's a collection behind for the Finance Supplement and the buildings and the clothes will look very good together. Forget the interview. He's probably really boring and, anyway, who's going to know him? Just put backdrops in – 'Buildings: de Winter Associates', like they were an accessory. And use some catchy words – 'SkyHigh', 'Dare!', 'Money Walks', that kind of thing. And hey – don't worry'.

So Arabella – a ready-bottled cocktail of emotions and shaken, if not stirred, by her meeting – walked slowly back to her office and marvelled at the capriciousness of creative management whose ways are sometimes strange but generally for the best.

Max de Winter looked at his reflection in the windows of a passing taxi on the Strand and thought he could see the slightly widening eyes of a diver whose pool had just transformed into a parquet of tessellating television screens. Trafalgar Square was baking, and London drowsed heat-stupid through the silent overture to Max de Winter's funniest lines in that brief comedy, his life.

Two: Her New CD

Gemma Danvers emerged from a precocious Chelsea childhood spent in a Sydney Street cottage surrounded by expensive cornflower-blue bric-à-brac to learn the necessity of involvement. Not being of a philanthropic inclination, she avoided the organising of charity balls in favour of becoming a creative consultant to the media set. Her greatest work of art was her diary, which bulged with useful telephone numbers, the correct arrangement of which could see her through one hectic day to the next, and so on, until one day she would either get married, become her own boss, or die.

The result of all this involvement was difficult to quantify. Gemma was not like Arabella for she possessed neither the clever ear-rings made of coat hangers nor the dynamo of a careerist hysteria to make Malcolm Houston take her seriously. What she did have, other than her job on *Designate*, was a mantelpiece obscured by invitations and a greater degree of self-confidence than many people of her age, which was nineteen. It was a combination of her age, self-confidence, and fluency in business-speak as a second language that attracted Paul Vince, the fast-lane publicity person of Max de Winter Associates.

Once Gemma had jilted the muscle-bound synthesist of a well-known and generally disliked pop group, who had been paying her some attention for the previous three months, she and Paul commenced to eat their way across London. There were few weekends between May and October when the sedimentary hours of daylight were not washing the bonnet of Paul's BMW as it drifted between Maida Vale and Chelsea to pick up Gemma and nose back into twinkling Knightsbridge for a few hours serious eating.

The weekday routine was slightly different, weekdays being work-based and week evenings being the nutritious dessert to the main course of nine-to-six involvement.

It was by way of a social dessert that Paul and Gemma came to be at the eagerly anticipated private view of Dane

Aston's New Works in Bronze at Rebecca de Winter Fine Art Ltd in Cork Street.

By six thirty that evening the three spacious galleries were temporary workbench, weapon and tomb to nearly three hundred of the People Who Thought They Counted and about one hundred and fifty of their 'friends'. Here and there amongst the crowd some spaces were found to exhibit the spindly and esoteric New Works in Bronze that were the excuse for all the fuss. The bronzes themselves brought mixed comment – when they provoked any – and this uncertainty of opinion was due to some doubt over the generosity of their Meaning. The debt to Caro was generally considered immense.

Rebecca de Winter herself was thought to be fetching in watered silk, but having disturbed the rhythm of her Boston Fibre Diet with several glasses of Spanish champagne and two tranquillisers she looked on moodily as the bombastic and overdressed Aston became more and more noisily grateful for the nasal whoops of insincere congratulation that were being showered upon him by London's cognoscenti.

Around the slightly bow legs of *Autonomon 3* (1985) a small cluster of elderly painters were shouting tactless comments about both the artist and his work before turning round as one to beam roguishly into the white flare of a society reporter's camera flash.

Discovering that the white sauce in his vol-au-vent contained anchovies, the publicly vegetarian critic from *Art Digest* wedged its offensive remains between the narrow angles of what he later described as one of Aston's delicately shifting planes. Having wiped some crumbs out of his beard he wondered whether it was boredom or wine that was making his eyes water as he listened to an enthusiastic young sculptor explain to him how long he had been looking at lines and what excitement they caused him.

Angus Fythe-Brown (Grindlay's – Old Bond Street; Aquarelles and XIXth Century Fine Drawings) retired injured after being elbowed into the lethal corner of *Piece 5* (1986) by the wildly gesticulating Berta Hilsop, a Dutch buyer of little self-control who was engaged in a tearful and sisterly reconciliation with Andrea Hodgson of Sotheby's after nearly five months' unpleasantness over Paul Whitely's photolithographs.

The girl with the crudités cried quietly to herself in a corner subsequent to a suggestion put forward to her by the only person in the room who could claim to having known Cocteau.

Rebecca felt as though she were drowning. Her head ached and her arms were puckered with nervous shivering. She smiled weakly at Dane and then went into her office.

Just as she was groping for the door handle she overheard the triumphant roars of merriment coming from Paul Vince as he explained with the use of *Twin Locking Piece 2* (1985) that the enormous bronze hemispheres that were the hallmark of Aston's later work in fact displaced their centre of gravity to within a centimetre of collapse.

'Bloody thing can hardly stand up!' he crowed, the wine

inspiring him to a devil-may-care irreverence for his surroundings.

As Rebecca looked anxiously at the trembling structure of several thousand pounds worth of unsold art – that least stable of commodities – she happened to catch Gemma's eye, and Gemma, not being a girl to miss a professional opportunity, immediately snatched at the chance of a chat.

'I hear you've left your husband again,' boomed the jovial Gemma with a tactlessness that echoed all the way to the Royal Academy.

'I hardly think that's any of your business,' replied Rebecca, dipping the barbs of her words into the liquid poison of pure politeness – a technique entirely wasted on the cast-iron sensibilities of the self-assured Chelsea-bred Gemma Danvers.

'Well, he won't let *Designate* interview him, which you can imagine is perfectly bloody ghastly for poor old Arabella who got landed with the feature. Seems rather odd to me – rude not to, I'd have thought, but the editor's more or less lost interest now anyway. Is he still designing those weird buildings? My sister's boyfriend used to arbitrate in one of them or something and he's a real laugh. I'm completely useless with anything to do with money. Where did you get your shoes? I've been looking for some like that for ages.'

'You must excuse me,' said Rebecca, 'I'm very busy this evening.'

'Is it drugs?' queried Gemma as the office door closed. 'I mean, one hears so much about drugs these days, and . . . '

Rebecca retired into her office, and Gemma giggled as

Paul bit her neck. Together they descended the steps of Rebecca de Winter Fine Art and stumbled off down Cork Street, returning art to its customary place between Lifestyle and Contacts on the priority scale of their professional requirements.

Closing the door on the clamour in the gallery, Rebecca lay down on the floor of her office, a worn-out mermaid beached on watered silk. She picked up the telephone and dialled New Manderley, gently massaging the back of her neck with her free hand as she listened to the ringing tone. There was no reply. Maybe it was too early, or maybe Max was still in London. There had been a rumour that he was about to design a night club and Rebecca recalled the three notices that were hanging above premises in New Burlington Street. One sign said (in gold): 'The Al Hambara Club'. Beneath that sign a further notice said: 'The Most Exclusive Wining and Dining Nightspot in London' and beneath that a smaller, slightly shabby sign said: 'Lease for Sale'. It would be like Max for him to be prowling around the dark and dusty innards of a closed-down nightspot working out how to rebuild it. But Max would never design another building. She felt sure of it. And what was a 'nightspot' anyway? It sounded like an ugly blemish that appears on the face of a city that lives unhealthily after dark.

Rebecca hung up and poured herself some sour coffee from the percolator in her secretary's office. Then she got her cigarettes out of her desk drawer and lay down on the floor again. Outside she could hear the private-view guests saying things they didn't mean like 'See you later on!' and 'Hope you can make it!'

She stared at the telephone, the room cool and dark around her. She had locked the door.

Her office felt like a sepulchre made out of tungsten, and she wanted only for a griffin, or a journalist, to curl up with a Bible at her feet to enable her to do an imitation of a lady by her knight in a tomb.

The side chapel of the Collegiate Church of St Jude in the village of Ashby-cum-Manderley contained such a pair of eternally resting aristocrats. Sixteenth-century. Max adored that church. In a niche in the adjacent wall of the chapel, hollowed out of the kindly sandstone, there was another smaller tomb underlined with memorial verse where was laid the departed earl's noble impe. Apparently impes were lucky in the sixteenth century, an ancient precursor of having a hairdresser you can trust.

Max and Rebecca de Winter had never been very good at the Country Life, despite Max's increasing obsession with the Glorious Heritage of England. Watching his interrogation of English History was like watching someone trying to cook on ice. The greater the fire of his passion for the subject, the more the subject itself dissolved, and his meditations by hedgerows and riverbanks seemed to bring nothing but frustration and sadness.

Soon after they were married Max and Rebecca de Winter had decided to have an 'At Home'. On the appointed day the rain poured down across the garden, and through the open windows you could hear the cedar drip. The sun came out. It started raining again. The guests were amused to see the perfect couple so unprepared for the reality of their quaint idea.

In the evening after the guests had gone, Max and Rebecca left the house to let some air blow the perfume and cigar smoke away and went for a walk along the cliff tops. Max was in thoughtful mood, calculating the height of a ceiling or the depth of a lift shaft. Leaving him to his own thoughts, Rebecca had wandered off on her own down the cliff path that led to a little cove.

Max was inexplicably angry with her for doing this.

'I told you not to go down there,' he snapped. 'It's just a stretch of sand – an old boat house. There's nothing to see.'

Rebecca tensed at his outburst, slipping her fingers through the collar of their labrador. 'I'm sorry darling,' she replied, her eyes bright with tears. 'I was looking for a rope for Jasper. I didn't mean to annoy you.'

Max de Winter was a difficult man.

A crimson sunset fell across the wet lawn, drawing long black shadows from the house and the trees. The garden walk dripped and the apple blossom hung low under its heavy cargo of rainwater. Down on the beach wet shells lay warming in the last of the sun, their tiny serrated edges tracing delicate patterns in the surf-hammered sand. Max de Winter was wondering just how many wrong trees there were for a dog to bark itself hoarse beside, and saw in this canine error a ventriloquism of his own situation. Confused architect put on trial by the purpose of his profession. Architect unsettled by love, buildings, London and his times. Architect takes horrible revenge by quitting

– wife and colleagues upset and confused. A salt breeze flicked at his hair; he took off his jacket and rolled up his sleeves before turning to smile at Rebecca, and ask her forgiveness for his temper. But Rebecca had gone, walking along quickly ahead of him to go and sit by herself somewhere and consider what kind of a life she was living.

Max de Winter's fame after the success of his Pacman Software building had been considerable. The nylon touch of cruel irony was on the fact that it was to be his penultimate building.

The following morning, on the tube to his office so far away from the seabord garden of the previous evening, Max considered the stickiness of his fame. Silent fame for a silent profession. Nobody ever heard architects speak. Not really. 'Max de Winter,' he said to himself. 'Spray it on dry hair and the style will stay there; spray it on wet hair . . . and one supposes that nothing much will happen.' He repeated these absurdities to himself, litany-like, all the way to Mansion House station.

Rebecca realised that she was still staring at the telephone and dialled New Manderley again, lighting a cigarette and balancing her shallow white coffee cup from the Contemporary Crafts Gallery on the bevelled edge of her compressed-rubber studio table.

At the other end of the call, at New Manderley, Max was writing a list. It read:

D'Arblays Trust

Self & Assurance

Pacman Software plc

The Museum of Corporate Finance
The Church of God the Truth (Tower Hill)
Margate?

He was sitting at a little table in the billiard room of New Manderley. The furniture was covered in dust sheets. Outside it was threatening thunder again.

Max stared at the list and numbered his buildings from one to five. He felt sentimental about the hacienda in Margate. A door slammed upstairs, caught in the draught from an open window. Rain began to thud against the windows. Max realised that if he took off his dark glasses he would be able to see better. He left them on.

A dream lay waiting in the out-tray of his mind. He pictured Rebecca, his pretty young wife, running her fingers through her hair. She is sitting on the ancestral hearth, there at New Manderley, and she is wearing a ball gown. She rubs the front of her legs, staring into the fire that is heating her taffeta.

'I'm so confused,' she says, her chin trembling slightly but her soft voice bravely even.

Max feels a hot sensation in his stomach. He lights a pipe, pressing the hot tobacco down with his thumb. He exhales some smoke, looks at the ceiling, and coughs. The newspaper slips off his knees and he goes over to turn the wireless down. Rebecca is crying softly by the fire. Sobbing. Her tears are dissolving her eyeliner.

Max says, 'I can't bear to see you crying on the hearth again.' Rebecca desperately wants to run into his arms. Somehow she can't. She wants Max to comfort her, but he looks so far away, he looks like a stranger! He wants to do something helpful. If he comes any closer to her she'll scream.

'L'Amour Fou,' Rebecca whispers, despite herself, 'Lee Miller . . . '

'Darling, don't cry. Please don't . . . '

Rebecca buries her face in her hands. The firelight glows in her hair. She is so terribly alone. So terribly misunderstood. She is the victim of so many cruel sensations that obscure the way between happiness and herself. Max panics, uncertain of how to calm her. He tries changing the subject.

'I've decided to blow up my complete works, darling,' he says in the same tone of voice one would use to say 'We're going to move to Tuscany.'

Anticipating incomprehension, the dream flicks a succession of images through Max's mind: Lincoln's Inn Fields, chocolate croissants, a jar of moisturiser, a painting by Steven Campbell. Then the dream refocused, disaster threatening.

'Oh Max!' Rebecca wails, twisting the hot hem of her dress. Her voice is husky and confused. Max can feel his heart knotting with grief and self-loathing. A nervous nausea creeps through his system like a mini cab lost in south London. He wants to love her so much, to take her tiredness home, kinder than God . . . He whistles noiselessly.

'My Bonny lies over the sea . . . '

There is thunder directly overhead. And then everything happens at double speed. There is a sudden crack and the high-pitched war cry of a low-flying cinder as it hurls itself into the folds of Rebecca's ball-gown. The dress catches fire.

Max leaps up in his dream and throws his pipe into a far corner of the hall, cursing Jasper for going off obediently to retrieve it.

He drags Rebecca from the blazing wreckage of her dress, beating off quadrants of smoking taffeta before the flames can reach her lingerie.

As he carries her up the moonlit staircase to her room he despises himself for announcing his vandalistic intentions towards his buildings. Why can't he control himself? That this should happen! It must be a sign, the gods drumming their fingers on the conference table by way of an omen of imminent tragedy.

The dream slinks darkly off, throwing a spiteful glance over its shoulder to the waking Max. The telephone was ringing in the next room.

Answering it, Max nearly wept to hear Rebecca's tired voice.

'I was having such a strange dream,' he said, 'and I must tell you about it. Please – will you come down?' There was a pause.

'I'm rather busy,' replied Rebecca. 'It's the opening of Dane's show and I ought to be here.'

'I'm not going back to the office, Rebecca. I'm giving up . . . architecture.' There was another pause.

'Why?'

'I'm simply finished. With it. Someone wanted to interview me. It broke something. I don't want to be here any more. I don't want to leave my buildings behind either.'

'What do you mean?'

'Please come back, Rebecca. If only for a day. I don't want you to hate me any more.'

'I don't hate you.'

'I don't want you to be indifferent to me. I want you to be happy. I know I can't make you happy but I wish we could understand one another again. Just once. We once said we loved one another more than we loved life itself . . .'

' . . . and now we're going to die anyway,' finished Rebecca.

The rain was hammering on the windows as Max de Winter sat hunched over the phone. In the garden the magnolia was luminous against the night.

'Will you come down?' asked Max.

'Not now,' said Rebecca, 'but I still love you . . . in some ways. Maybe when things are a bit quieter here in a month or two. I'd better go. Are you all right?'

'No,' replied Max.

And they hung up, their conversation terminated by the planned obsolescence clause that was written into their marriage contract. This was the clause of poetry, and poetry is the soul's dartboard, the place where the feelings stick in. Never theirs the door jamb to varnish or the bird-table to mend.

Estrangement, anxiety and terrorism crept silently into the service of Max and Rebecca de Winter's ambitions for a happy marriage.

Rebecca sighed and wondered whether she should,

after all, go down and see Max. She decided against it. She looked in her bag for a lighter and a receipt fluttered out on to the floor. She remembered that she had bought a compact disc player at lunch time.

2

PSYCHOWHIZZIOLOGY

One: Party Games from New Manderley

THE CEMENT dust and petrol fumes of an August after-noon in Charlotte Street mingled with the scent of Arabella Cloth's Rhubarb and Jojoba Midday Tone-Up Lotion as the *Designate* profile team grouped earnestly round the conference table to discuss their feature on Max de Winter.

Malcolm Houston was in a particularly creative mood, having just lunched around the corner with an exciting and new ceramicist from the RCA. Although largely mono-syllabic in her conversation Debbi Tring could do radical things with glaze, and her latest 'holocaust' breakfast china was causing quite a stir in artistic and commercial circles alike. Picking moodily at her devilled mushroom mousse, Debbi had given Malcolm all that he needed for an enthusiastic paragraph in the *Designate* 'Next Up' pages.

On the subject of de Winter he addressed the meeting as follows: 'You people – ah – have maybe been aware that we've not had much – that is not 100 per cent co-operation from de Winter Associates – on this – ah – one, and I – ah – must admit that my gut hunch was to ah – drop it.'

As one the *Designate* team looked concerned about the hunch but simultaneously optimistic about the replacement suggestion that their editor's raised eyebrows were forcing them to anticipate.

'It would seem,' he continued, 'that we alone are left to tell the tale, but I'll ask Arabella to fill you in on the background.' There was a low fizz like pressurised bilgewater being squirted out of the side of a ship as Gemma opened a bottle of Perrier.

'Thanks Malcolm,' whispered Arabella, in a committed kind of way. 'As you have probably heard, Max de Winter is not available for an interview so we're going to be relying on the visuals as both a comment on Max the man and as a backdrop for the fashion that Betty's putting together. As regards the shoot, we're going to begin at D'Arblays Trust in Moorgate. The main arbitration floor and home accounts offices. I have some pictures here of the interiors and as you can see they're really very new and exciting.' Some glossy prints of what looked like the back of a clock and some carpet squares were circulated to the meeting. Murmurs of interest, enthusiasm, commitment, optimism, and excitement were duly forthcoming.

'We're using the same model agency that we had for the Soho Facelift feature, and Betty has got winter collections from MythMyth, Henry Kong and Margot Jones. The shoot is next Tuesday' (a noise like a house falling down accompanied the opening of thirteen diaries), 'and it's at nine in the evening. From D'Arblays we're doing Self & Assurance on Thursday night; the Church of God the Truth – that'll be a sportswear spread – in Tower Hill on Friday after evening purification; Pacman Software plc over the week-end; and The Historic Invoices Library the following Monday – that's almost in the Docklands so Gemma's checking we're not double-booked with anyone else.' She paused, sucking the end of her mapping pen thoughtfully. 'Malcolm?'

'Thanks, Arabella. Now, cover stars. We've finally got hold of one old picture of Max de Winter that we think is really good. It's old but it looks – archaic.' He held up a black-and-white photograph of Max taken some years before. He is standing on the steps of an office block wearing a long gabardine trench coat. His face is smiling and his hair is short and neat for the mid-seventies. He is wearing a pair of dark glasses.

The meeting dispersed.

The following evening Max de Winter was sitting on the steps of the Royal Exchange. His hair was uncombed, greased back behind his ears, and his face was drawn and tired. Lukewarm drizzle gusted across the street and his raincoat was flecked with little black spots. One of his shoes was unlaced. Hovering overhead, the sun was too red, and as a car sped by, its wheels hissing on the wet road, Max looked at the City as one would study a putrefying piece of fruit. It was eight forty-five.

He grimaced, and then got up carefully. His chest was

aching even more than usual and as usual he ascribed the pain to nerves.

His car, an old Ford Granada bought for cash that afternoon, was parked down a side street. Inside it was a large quantity of high explosive.

Very gently he got into the car and turned on the ignition, waiting for a moment before driving off slowly into the gathering darkness wherein the Self & Assurance London headquarters was towering.

The windscreen wipers pulled across the windscreen making a horrible rubbing noise. Max felt lonely. He thought of the crowds that happily filled these streets during the day, and of how he had never been of their number, not even when he used to meet Rebecca for lunch at St Paul's.

Soon he was opposite the building that had won him a medal from his colleagues. He was just twenty-six when some Captain of Industry snipped the ribbon, and he still hated him for it.

'Welcome to the Labelling Conference,' whispered Max to the night as he got out of the car and tiptoed over to the darkened doorway of a newsagents from where there was a good view of the edifice of white metal and granite that was to be his first victim.

Leaning against the shop door, Max remembered with a lump in his throat how Rebecca and he had co-designed the tiles for the men's room of the banking section. Fishbones and Mexican eyes, quaint hieroglyphs that meant nothing at all to the staff who used the facilities they decorated. Why, Max and Rebecca had even supervised the grouting. It had been a labour of love. And then there were the directors' rooms on the twelfth floor, the brick-work faced with specially corroded metal sheets and rusted bolts salvaged from old ships cleverly adapted as light fittings. 'Ruins in Action', the *Urbanist* critique had stated. 'The Triumph of Trashing', roared an American commentary.

Then darker thoughts came into Max's mind, and it was hard to know in the fading twilight whether the walls of the Self & Assurance were exhaust-stained or in shadow. Once they had been white, tinted anniversary silver that time mellowed into a slightly sluttish daughter of pearl. But now these white walls were definitely brown, turning to a teak of mediocrity that recalled the tragic bridal suite where Rebecca and he had attempted a second honey-moon. On the second night Max had smashed an after-shave bottle against the flock on the wall and then sunk slowly to the foot of the enormous bed on which Rebecca lay with her tear-brimming eyes wide open. They had drowned on land at that coastal resort because of architec-ture and neurosis and some insidious bad magic that always put them out of one another's reach, incapable of giving happiness, or strength, or confidence, or support.

A cold breeze whipped around the corner of Self & Assurance and dark clouds billowed into the summer sky. The moon was new and exciting, a brilliant star twinkling to one side of it.

Lighting a cigarette, Max dreamt for a moment of how the eyes and head and heart could roam these streets with nothing but vandalism in mind. Let his terrorism, he thought, though empty of compassion, not be devoid of meaning. After the scarlet of evening had turned into the purple prose of night and all around was sleep or sleeplessness, Max wanted the Self & Assurance building to become some kind of ship of the line, pitched between the horns of a dilemma by force. And in an upstairs room somewhere, by candlelight, under beams or rafters, tarred or scented, Max knew that the unbelievably ghostly She would be sleeping on the hearth rug again. It was during these short aromatic nights that Max might very well die, and seeing how he had lost his way and his wife, separated from silk by suit, he hoped she would quickly forget him. And with that thought he quickly walked back over to the car, turned on the ignition and wedged the accelerator down. The he ran for cover.

Ten seconds later a sheet of flame spat former building through the roar of a massive explosion. Windows blew out in all directions and the shattered ergonomic fixtures of a major financial institution arched fitfully into the street. The first three floors were gutted and, as the main frame of the building weakened, whole panels of plaster, steel, brick and rubber plant came tumbling down into the charred remains of the foyer.

Feeling in his raincoat pocket, Max took out two grenades and hurled them into the rubble. One blew the mailing room apart and the second transformed a vending machine into so much powdered plastic. Shards of open plan screening came fluttering down from a great height, some still trailing memos or holiday postcards. The lift shafts were ablaze and scarlet flames licked lasciviously out of many of the windows. On the roof the wigwam water tank was steaming.

As sirens and bells began to fill the air Max climbed neatly over a wall down the street and dropped into the car park of a neighbouring office.

Getting into his E-Type, his mind was full of nothing. He felt bored, or numb, or nothing at all. He drove west towards the Strand, then parked in Covent Garden to try and find somewhere to have a cup of coffee amongst the purgatorial Piazza hell-hole cafés and wine bars. Above the merry lights of Covent Garden hung the life of indecision like broken veins, and the bloodshot crescent of the moon, staring moodily into the middle distance, was brooding on red.

The emergency services were still finding pulped box files and buckled work stations amongst the smoking ruins of the Self & Assurance London headquarters as Arabella Cloth, forced into a peculiar mood by the speed with which a magazine feature could be transformed into an omelette of broken masonry, locked herself into her office to have a lonely and unprofessional little cry.

She wasn't sure what had prompted her tears or why they should fall in such profusion. She changed her multivitamin course and finally stopped drinking coffee. She looked with a kinder eye upon the socially dyslexic Gemma. She softened.

'I think maybe I'm not getting enough zinc,' she said in a broken voice to her gay flatmate, Jim.

'I thought that it was iron that made people moody,' he

answered, brewing her a beaker of parsnip and privet tea, the paper label on the bag of which contained a thousand-word history of herbal nerve tonics, beginning with Saxon root infusions and then passing glibly over Victorian patent medicine, acknowledging the discovery of hysteria with a respectful nod before admitting with shy pride that the tea about to be drunk had been blended with the massed herb research of the last eight hundred years. Arabella would have to, surely, benefit.

Arabella swallowed a mouthful of the orange boiling liquid and her lips puckered, her cheeks sucked in and her throat fizzed viciously, the delicate flooring of her stomach buckling in panic by way of warning to the bowel.

'Oh God, that's good!' she croaked, and lit a cigarette.

Arabella had stopped by the cordoned-off bomb site earlier that afternoon. It was raining. In the shallow crater a few policemen in high-visibility vests had been picking their way through the bureaucratic entrails that the explosion had thrown up.

She asked if she could take some pictures and this had been refused. Not having the strength to argue, she had thanked them anyway in very slow English and pretended to be a tourist. From the papers and the television it was clear that nobody had accepted responsibility for the 'outrage'.

They rescheduled the fashion shoot. They would delay publication of the de Winter feature. They would try to interview some terrorists and maybe run their findings across the camouflage textiles and swimwear photographs that they had been trying to place.

Nobody could get through to de Winter Associates. A secretary – or it could have been an ansafone – patiently explained to callers in a soft American accent that there was nobody there right now but, hey, thanks for calling anyway. There was no tone, and no invitation to leave a message. The spectral secretary just kept on showing you the door with a smile.

Gemma had not heard from Paul Vince either. She didn't really mind that much because she had recently decided that she didn't really like him anyway and furthermore she had met Rupert D'Oyle ffookes, currently in his second term at Sandhurst and a real laugh in the chukka. Through the oily Rupert Gemma had learned her new expression, 'Bloody funny', followed by an appreciative widening of the facial muscles, and it was this habit that caused Malcolm Houston to pause in the middle of picking fluff out of the turn-ups of his Japanese trousers and consider giving Gemma the boot. He decided against it.

It was about a week later, when Malcolm and Arabella were sifting through the hundreds of CVs that *Designate* received every week from hopeful contributors, that a newsflash on Malcolm's Watchman alerted them to a new tragedy in the City of London.

' . . . and read Combined Media and Communication Studies at Grimsby Polytechnic from 1985 to . . . ' Malcolm read in a weary voice like one condemned to memorise the Yellow Pages. His reading was interrupted by the urgent voice of the newsflash.

'Reports are coming in of a further attack on one of the City's leading investment agencies. D'Arblays Trust, a brokerage house on London Wall, was severely damaged earlier this evening by what the police are calling a copy-cat attack of the crude car bomb that destroyed the Self & Assurance headquarters in the City earlier this week. There have only been a few minor injuries and this the police are describing as "miraculous".'

Malcolm looked at Arabella, the carefully typed CV hanging limply in his hand. 'Another of de Winter's,' he said slowly, and then Arabella burst into tears again.

Whilst Arabella wrung a boutique tissue between her fingers and Malcolm Houston rang some friends in the City, Max de Winter sat quietly on the river wall by Traitor's Gate and felt no remorse at all about his latest attack on his career. He had no doubts at all about the bastard yuppies whom he had just made homeless; they were stinking vagrant zombies for whom he felt neither sympathy nor compassion. They just got in the way, but would survive, regardless of the ferocity of the de Winter campaign of violence.

'I should leave London for good,' thought Max, 'leave for some provincial town this autumn, some place of historic interest and natural beauty that is the loose change rattling about in history's charity box. To Manderley perhaps, and the Collegiate Church of St Jude, by way of 'B' roads and dual carriageways under white expressionless skies, fringed with August bracken.

'Here lies Max de Winter
Architect, Husband and Terrorist.
We by example are warned and mourn
His Going on Ahead to a Higher Choir.'

A twenty-one gun tone from a battery of desk-top PCs, crossed RIBA *Journals* at dawn, the futile vigil, the insincere hymns and the golden gargoyles – the stupid image and ridiculous fancy. It had been easier to blow up D'Arblays than he had thought. A fire alarm set off, the assembling of a few late night workers in the car park and their ho-ho decision to go to the Chip and Cheese for a few drinks . . . The ease with which Max had parked a brand new Golf under the smoked-glass porch with the bronze finishing that had been called 'provocative'. The time bomb amongst the packs of explosives on the back seat, the run for cover. The discovery – at last – of an issue of *Designate* amongst the dustbins where Max had hidden. He was halfway through the Rome supplement when D'Arblay's went up a few minutes later. A small explosion, then an enormous one; a waterfall of glass and a few screams. Max finished the Nightlife paragraph and then peered out to inspect the damage. The explosives had been supplied by a no-questions man who demolished old council flats during the day. It must have been extremely powerful. Max was amazed when he saw that the fourth floor – Overseas Accounts and Direct Budgeting – had shifted in more or less one piece some fifty metres down the street and crushed several small shops and a

Rocco sandwich bar upon landing. This meant that the fifth and sixth floors, concertinaing the lift shafts, had become as one with the lobby, and the intervening floors were therefore compressed into a kind of layer cake out of which electric cables spat sparks and little fires flickered through the dust. Further baby explosions puffed clouds of black smoke into the night. Here and there a desk slid out of a window or a filing cabinet crashed through a wall.

As the moment hung stretched and dazed, Max lay full length behind his dustbin. Night was falling when the police arrived, the blue lights on their vans and cars washing in circles around the street. The bomb squad, ambulances, the press – all the relevant bodies gathered Lilliputian around the wrecked financial institution, and Max cracked a grin. The grin soon went and Max followed after it, going down to the river to sit by Traitor's Gate and ponder the success of his attack.

He considered the mess left over on history's palette by the vigorous and neurotic process of keeping the masterpiece of the urban centre alive with these inspired acts of terrorism. He walked through Lincoln's Inn Fields, smoking a cigarette and feeling his invisibility. He was fading a little more with each building destroyed, crossing out his signature on the skyline with his bare hands, the same bare hands with which he had built a glittering career and sculpted an envied marriage. Irony, the liquid engineering within the machinery that drove Max de Winter as myth, leant a pleasing symmetry to the otherwise arbitrary and chaotic bombardment of man by phenomena that was the reality of Max the Man.

At one in the morning, dozing in front of a glass of vodka in the conservatory at New Manderley, Max turned his clouded mind to the destruction of Pacman Software plc, but was aware only of a palm frond fluttering in the sea breeze that stroked his jungle logic – the life after love and success, the melodrama of an everyday failure whose imagination was teaching emotional karate to be used for self-destructive purposes. What a way to go.

Despite the upper and lower case 'i's, life goes on regardless. This may be annoying in itself, the individual determined to beg a crisis or statement off the general indifference of Time to a lonely and bitter old soul. Whatever it is that psychology does – knocking down buildings or selling magazines, marrying people or murdering them – it would seem that the universe shrugs. All this high drama, the tiny details in pink and grey or black and white that cluster like summer insects about the slow afternoon of memories – in all this is the meaningless statement, the difficult to translate. And so strenuous singles are played after tea at New Manderley, house-party games going on and on amongst laughter or silent rage. Happy families, whist and vandalism, the endless charade of watching the roof fall in, and finally, before dinner, or before sleep, or raising a ragged cheer as in some inexplicably hilarious way we witness the house falling down – with or without the aid of explosives.

Two: Pacman Software plc

'THERE'S A GHOST IN MY HOUSE'

It was early afternoon, the second Friday in August. From the upstairs windows of New Manderley, the yellowing fields were shimmering under a heat haze and the trees in the middle distance appeared cross-hatched by sunlight and shadows. A heavy stillness filled the air, the only sounds being a dove that cooed beneath the eaves and the far-off booming of the sea. Fleshy pink roses hung limply around the windows, and after Max had breathed in their scent he exhaled with an expressive sigh that combined immense longing with deep regret, the respiratory equivalent of a requiem.

This was the weekend that Max had set aside to blow up his finest building. These were the leisure hours during which Pacman Software plc, that symphony in polished granite, was destined to reach its final crescendo, the dusk of Sunday evening set to play host to the last few echoing chords of the explosion, a handful of delicate arpeggios in shattered glass playing out the emotional coda.

Pacman Software was the building that Max de Winter considered to be the Bride of All Loveliness, the girl he never married and could therefore never leave. In its thirty-five floors of carefully designed workspace, from the lyrical Italian marble of the lobby to the Californian aluminium cladding of its roof-top solar panels, Max saw only beauty, and when he gazed into the smoky sheets of windows it was his soul that he saw reflected there.

Designate magazine was also scheduled to work over the weekend of 10 and 11 August – booked into Pacman Software to take some fashion photographs.

By Friday lunch time the heat was in residence, and the streets around Cannon Street were soon bursting at their wine bars with relaxed City workers all loosening their striped collars and looking forward to the weekend. From the Buying Department of Pacman Software about twenty of the younger staff had congregated outside The Olde Lampe and Firkin to generally have a bit of a laugh. By 1 p.m. most things were 'bloody funny', 'you know really', and laughter began to spill out at the slightest joke as jackets were taken off and sleeves rolled up to the fierce heat of the sun.

Angus Treadleigh, fired with a passion for Diana in Shipping, over at Lampwert Beazeley, the marine insurance people, gazed happily around at his laughing colleagues and thought with pleasure about the interest his well invested money was earning him even as he laughed. He had just bought a two-bedroomed flat down river and things were looking set for a weekend of suntan oil and sex on the secluded oven of a balcony that his brilliantly negotiated mortgage had secured for him as a feature of his purchase.

The depth of the pleasure came from imagining just the merest hints of what might swim across his week-end. A fridge door swinging open to catch Diana's face with a blast of light and watercress-scented cool, the darkness of a shadow off a new concrete wall at five in the afternoon with a clear sky above it, the lazy drowse of passing pleasure boats in the evening.

At New Manderley Max de Winter sweated as he loaded dynamite into the back of his car. He would sleep in his old office on Friday night and wire up Pacman early Saturday morning. He was going to pretend to be doing a structural survey of the building – as its architect this seemed only natural.

Friday's dusk was particularly idyllic, a bunch of black grapes being slowly burst in the mouth of London. Early evening was a harmony of brakelights and relaxed pedestrians, the golden blue of the West End washing gently against the white cliffs of Bloomsbury. Arabella Cloth strolled down Charlotte Street with nothing in mind but a dinner *à deux* with boyfriend Nick, a sandy-haired sculptor of immense talent whom the system had forced to be a pushbike messenger, complete with greased pony-tail and shoulder-high walkie-talkie. They would dine in silence, surrounded by the orange-blossom tenting of her bed, all curiosity about media, art and exploding buildings pushed to one side with the ice bucket.

Rupert would spend the evening alone in his darkroom, flipping the channels on a two-inch-screen TV and rereading Lyotard as an intellectual work-out. Gemma was powdering her neck in preparation for a South Kensington ball, Paul Vince's orchids already filed in the pedalbin and her grandmother's engagement brooch demurely pinned to her dress.

Angus of Pacman Buying (International) was cleaning his bath and watching the cable. His New Age CD plinked and plunked with a suitably ambient eeriness in his minimalist living room and beside the *Investor's Chronicle* a copy of *Easy Money*, a novel by Steven Hinksmith, lay open at a raunchy bit. Glancing at a page as he passed by to Windolene his mirror Angus read: 'He saw her nipples hardening beneath the soft silkiness of her blouse, suddenly the helicopter exploded . . . '. It was a fast-paced action thriller, all right for just before bed but a definite step down from *Dubrovsky's Chessmen*, the Kremlin exposé that Angus kept by for the tube.

Angus wondered long and hard about what Diana's nipples were like and then went to look in the fridge. He was a success.

Of all this cast of characters the only two left unoccupied were the two who linked them together, Max and Rebecca de Winter. Max was sitting in his old office, at his old desk, in his old desk chair. He felt old. He felt like a ghost. He could read the impression of his last memo on the charcoal-grey blotter on his desk – he just had to hold it up to the desk lamp:

'Burn the Files'.

Across the street, beneath the neo-Gothic minarets and cupola of a disciple of Pugin's attempt at Camelot, the windows of Wheatley & Vernham (Solicitors) glowed bronze in the twilight. The dusty offices were blind to Max's illicit presence, the mirror-glazing of the de Winter building keeping any onlookers out. This was a good thing, lending as it did an element of tactical anticipation to the design of Fortress Max.

Back in Cork Street Rebecca de Winter was alone in her

gallery. A large oil painting was propped up against the wall in front of her, and she walked up and down with a cigarette in her hand, stopping occasionally to look at it. It was *Pineapple Causality for Defoe* (1986) by Lawrence Crane, a new and exciting painter from Oxford whose art school attendance stretched halfway round the world from his foundation year at Athens Technical College to a divided Master's from the Slade in London and the Kunstschule in Hamburg. Twenty-six years of eclectic cultural influence were written into the deceptively easeful cartoon of chaos that the massive canvas depicted.

The painting took as its focal point a self-portrait of Crane. By applying the irony of Schwitters to the agony of Bacon and stirring in a hint of the Glasgow School Crane had depicted himself seated at a blue grand piano, the strings of which were cascading serpentine into the stagnant green foreground wherein they converted to longstemmed roses, florid of petal and vicious of thorn. The face of the 'pianist' was a mask of wild despair, brown eyes fixed psychotically upon the white and nervous fingers that were splayed across the red and purple keyboard. In the background a parade of jungle animals lurched, powder-blue elephants jostling yellow pelicans and wild snow tigers bounding hysterically into a paradoxically arctic sunset. Their highly comic forms were offset against a drape of blue velvet above which hung a shining motorbike, spokes like moonbeams and the gas tank buffed to a dull maroon. In the right-hand corner a country churchyard stood surrounded by verdant foliage. To the left an elegant ship passed away into tropical azure.

Rebecca tried to determine – in her own mind, for her sake – whether it was the role of nature that Crane was discussing in this allegory or the role of painting itself. She was sure, at any rate, that it was the quintessential Crane, and would certainly fetch the demanded thousands. There were no less than three requests to reserve it, and *FlashArt* was doing an interview. A Star was being Born, and everyone wanted a cut of the nutritional afterbirth.

Rebecca remembered the exploding sun that had been the birth of Max's stardom, the ceaseless attention and flattery, the 'he-can't-put-a-foot-wrong-everything-he-does-is-art' legend. All for being good-looking and an architect. All for being a person, moreover, who used to be happy – until the spotlight gave him sunstroke and changed into an inquisitor's blinding torch.

London never tires of success stories and why should it? Living as she had in the Green Room of Triumph, Rebecca knew by heart the discourse of Success and could follow the vapid annotations to Glamour like a script. The circuitry of Fame, the Souvenir issue – the intellectually italicised portfolio that was rushed out by the backers at the merest sniff of serious money.

In the absence of carefully marketed talent and the industry that thrived within its hinterland one could always consider the alternative option of the patronising classes which is the profession of banking. A boy with whom Rebecca had hidden in the back of a wardrobe at a children's party for her ninth birthday was now a commodity broker living in West Surrey. Perhaps that vivid incident of her pre-pubescent years had driven her to see only the madness of art-pimping or the madness of money-pimping as ways to a comfortable lifestyle. She was past caring anyhow and wondered with a quiet smile which bank her crazed genius husband was likely to vandalise next.

As Saturday dawned Pacman Software was wrapped in a deep warm mist, and high above its lightning conductors the golden sphere of the sun was destined to burn the sky into clear blue by mid-morning. Beside St Paul's a window slammed and the pigeons on the cathedral steps scattered up into a wheeling crescent that soon dispersed into the masonry beneath the dome. It was going to be a very hot day.

The air was thickening in the deserted streets, and by nine a.m. the heat was enough to give the impression of late afternoon. It was a day of permanent sunset, the eternal summer evening.

A helicopter touched down on the landing barge opposite Bankside Power Station, the heat muffling the noise of its blades. The pilot in short sleeves was obscured by the dancing white lights that dazzled on the surface of the water. From the air the City would have looked like desert canyons, the irregular slopes and plateaux of golden and silver roofing breaking off into black chasms of shadow in the depths of which were the streets, the piazzas, the squares and the alleys.

The west facade of Pacman Software was gently humming in the heat. The steel-caged air-conditioning units that stretched at regular intervals beneath the thirteenth floor windows looked like basking lizards, and as Max de Winter stood beside a green security door and squinted up at the summit of his building there was something malevolent about the presence of these wall-hanging fixtures. It was curious, he thought, that in order to win his personal war he was forced to lose every battle. For Max the loss of each building was a defeat – he had wanted his buildings to glorify the financial centre of the UK. He had wanted them to be architectural jewels in the crown of England, their design offsetting the virtues of a green and pleasant land, their aesthetic references intended to echo a proud historic legacy of English tradition. He had wanted to stay at New Manderley, his garden palace, safe in the knowledge that London carried on in his absence growing prosperous and noble within the buildings that he had designed before his thirty-second birthday. How pitifully naive. A sickness chilled him and a dread of the work he had done and the role that it played in New England as the kinky dungeon of London Style City and the Money Brothel of Britain where all the young executives smelt of stale fish and the sweat of progressive greed.

Downstream, Angus was dreaming of a swimming pool beside the black-sanded desert, only it was his old school again and he was getting all the answers right by simply memorising the possible answers and underlining them in red.

Carrying a heavy suitcase that contained a number of powerful small bombs that could be detonated individually or collectively by a thing like a TV control unit, Max let himself into Pacman Software.

The security men, two of them, had been informed the previous day that Max would be calling – informed, that is, by Max himself pretending to be a Personal Assistant. Checking their appointment book, they respectfully tipped their hats, suspicious for merely the look of the thing. Security men must look suspicious at all times yet are generally so bored that one can catch them out.

Max felt sure that he was virtually invisible anyway. Even as he stood in front of the wide reception desk and said 'I'm Max de Winter, the architect, you should have a note of my visit' he felt that he could be neither seen nor heard.

'We thought you were one of the other lot,' said the smaller guard by way of conversation. 'You look like a fashion person.'

Max turned back, puzzled. 'What fashion people?' But the guard was laughing, doubtless at the peculiar things that fashion people do, and so Max assumed that he was merely telling a security-guard-style joke.

First of all Max went into the mezzanine cloakroom. In the lilac-scented air and purple lighting he felt his head clear a little and carefully planted one of his bombs, or 'leeches' as they are known in Mafia circles, behind a roller towel unit. Pausing to wash his hands and water back his hair, he then pulled on some surgical gloves and made his way to the lift.

Getting out at the third floor he planted four more leeches at either end of the corridor, two in the office of J.K. Cartwright (Assistant Director Exhibitions) and two more around the base of a cheese plant in the Display Department typing pool.

On the sixth floor he carefully unscrewed a panel off one of the cooling ducts. The sun was savage by now against the windows and Max noted with pride the efficiency of the air conditioning. He was disoriented, however, by the mesmeric stripes of shadow that fell from the vertical fabric blinds, and looking down at his ankle-length cement-coloured raincoat he felt like a zebra in a cage. Lighting a cigarette, he taped two leeches inside the service box of the cooling duct and screwed the panel back on.

Feeling a little cavalier, he sauntered down to the large conference room that occupied the entire width of the east end of the sixth floor. On the large back wall hung a painting by Tom Vreeland, one of the lesser known but highly collectable members of the London School. It depicted Commerce in London, a twilit city scene of bus tops and umbrellas against the buildings of London. In the foreground a hunch-shouldered businessman stared accusingly out of the canvas and peered at Max from under the brim of his hat, round wire-framed glasses lending a trace of menace to his painted eyes. The painting was dated 1958, and its predominant collaging of grey and yellow was fragmented by snail-trails of white that were the beginnings of a Great British Downpour.

Max looked out of the window at the unnatural heat bouncing watery distortions off the rooftops of London and then fastened a bomb to either side of the Vreeland's frame and shrugged.

'What the discovery of oil painting was to the Venetians,' he whispered to himself through a cloud of cigarette smoke, 'let dynamite and remote control be to the Art of Max de Winter. And I'm not really sorry about the Vreeland.'

Three floors down the *Designate* team were setting up lights and breakfasting on fruit juice and tubs of Greek yoghurt. Over by the windows the models were being carefully installed in the MythMyth winter collection. Catching three of her twenty-seven bracelets in the wild foam of her newly acquired peroxide perm, Betty the fashion editor was having the Compulsory Professional Crisis, her skewer-like personality making kebabs out of the sensitive natures of those she so enjoyed to supervise.

Much moving and removing of people, lights, clothes and props later, the first fifty photographs were pronounced a mess. Three tall girls with the standard-issue white crewcuts had been photographed over and over lolling moodily against door-frames and marching with serious looks on their faces up and down the geometrical playground of the famous de Winter fourth-floor corridor with its lime green pillars and triangular scarlet floor tiles.

Dressed in short black denim skirts and stretched-out jersey jackets, three more girls were beginning to pose themselves in arrangements of business-surreality as assistants various threw cashmere overcoats and accounts ledgers at them for nearly two hours.

And then it was lunch, a short professional break for all the committed professional people before taking to the roof to do the Margot Jones leather leggings and topcoats. Soon the *Designate* team were standing in the ruins of a salad that had been their lunch.

Max de Winter was working fast now, running from

floor to floor depositing bombs in any and every available space – under desks, in wastepaper baskets, between books, under sinks and behind filing cabinets. Pacman Software plc was alive with dynamite.

Soon he was on the roof. Leaning over the low metal balustrade he could see the whole of London bask beneath the afternoon sun. The river curled slowly into the heat haze, and the peaks of Centre Point, the Euston Tower, the London Hilton and the funnels of Battersea Power Station were all clearly visible despite their one tone of powdered gun-metal blue. Just down the street Max could see the grooved facade of the NatWest tower, and behind him – sinking, he felt, into the warm asphalt – stood the complex steel knitting of the new Lloyds Building, pods a-quivering in the desolate heat as though they were fruits getting ready to drop.

The aluminium cladding of the solar panels could not be approached directly, so Max left his last four bombs on the cast-iron cradle that supported them. A hot wind buffeted off the roof structures and Max had to steady himself with one hand as he closed his terrorist's suitcase.

Hearing giggles, whoops and severely uttered little cries of warning of the approaching *Designate* team, Max quietly slid behind a water tank and then took the service lift down to the ground floor.

Nodding to the security guards as he signed himself out, Max casually strolled through the lobby and then went down to the street, suitcase empty and raincoat flapping in a sudden gust from the pavement air vents.

When to press the button? It didn't really matter – or did

it? Did he want to massacre the innocent fashion victims playing on the roof of his greatest building? Dancing on his grave? Somehow he had not got the stomach for killing them knowingly. He sat in his car and left the primed detonator unit winking silently on the seat beside him. He felt tired and the car was warm and airless. He dreamt.

Rebecca and he were children, playing in the garden of Rebecca's house. It seemed important that the house was Rebecca's house, not his house, or their house, and Max was most definitely a guest.

Rebecca was like a little princess from a children's picture book, and Max was the idiot boy in love with her. He loved her desperately but there was something, some fact that he knew about himself but could not tell her, that prevented him from loving her honestly, or openly. She loved him desperately in return, and was tortured by the fact that he could not really love her. Held apart by this discrepancy, Max and she still played together, loving one another as much as they could, in the garden of Rebecca's house.

It was a law of the dream that if Max ever got into Rebecca's house she would never be free of him, so they had to play in the garden.

To entertain her Max had put on a big bearskin, the bear's head over his head and the flat skin over his back. He plodded up the garden path, pretending to be a bear. The skin was terribly heavy, but it made Rebecca laugh so much to see him shuffling along that she helped carry the skin to ease its weight on him, dancing for joy at the game.

Finally they reached the door of Rebecca's house, Max's head and the bear's head resting on the step. And then Rebecca remembered that she must not let him into her house or she would never be free of him and his tormenting non-love. She said, 'Oh no you don't, if once you get inside I'll never be free of you' and dropped the skin back onto Max so that it crushed him to the path. The skin was hard like pine needles.

So then they played some more in the garden until, standing on the over-green lawn, Rebecca put her hands to her cheeks and said, 'I don't feel well. I feel ill . . . '

And Max said, 'I'll get you a glass of water' and ran off to fetch it.

Rebecca shouted, 'Don't go into my house! It isn't water that I want anyway it's love!' And Max replied, squirming uncomfortably, 'But *I* love you!'

Rebecca's anger and distress worked her little girl's face into awkward shapes. She screamed 'But you *don't* love me!' and then stooped down in her little long dress to pick three stones out of the flower-bed – hard, sharp, flat stones. She hurled them with all her strength at Max's face.

The first he caught, and then the second, but at the third he screamed, 'But you'll kill me . . . '

Waking, Max looked out of the car window and decided to leave the detonation until the building was empty. On Sunday morning there wouldn't even be security people there, just a few hot lines from the burglar alarms and smoke detectors to the nearest police station.

Waiting for the bomb to go off – that is, waiting to push

the button . . . In these twelve hours the malignant chemicals that had been harassing Max de Winter for the previous God knows how many years began to finally coagulate into a horrific compound, Gothic in its inventiveness to prophecy, depict and scare. From the moment when he awoke in his E-Type Max was aware of the seconds ticking by like a dripping narcotic; they brought nocturne, lullaby and nightmare, the dusk, night and dawn all gathering about Pacman Software and Max's soul to bring the two of them down.

Late on Saturday evening Max thought about his afternoon, and of the activities traditionally set aside for other people's Saturday afternoons. Other people – decent, ordinary, healthy, prosperous citizens, those whose troubles, even tragedies, were contained by the standard social machinery of sympathy, celebration over adversity and thanksgiving for deliverance. The handsome groom and the nervous bride, those proud parents happy to announce and the privately reacting friends there gathered, so public in their approval. The highway is well lit, the stops ahead pre-planned. The nervous bride as Lovely in White as Rebecca had been – those who had attended any of Max and Rebecca's weddings could confirm the latter's Loveliness in White. The bride's spirit was maybe leaning against the hot side of the hired Daimler, eyes vacant, or piercing, and smoking a Senior Service untipped right down to the stub. On a Saturday afternoon of intense heat, with dust dropping off the sandstone steeples of Surrey or Kent, so many other people could be happily getting on with the business of living whilst Max was waiting to destroy his tallest building, at the height, as it were, of his creative powers.

There was also the consideration of all those people whose careers and self-images had maybe been founded on a glimpse at Pacman Software. The aspirant young executives' first post-graduate yearnings for a Good Life in the City. Dreams of brilliant financial coups on Thursday afternoons whilst the dramatic weather bounced off the windows and the head of a financial wizard was bent inspired over the screen of his desk-top terminal.

Max de Winter resented his inability to continue, and doubly resented the perversity of his monied despair. True despair is supposedly the property of the damned have-nots – it was galling as a have who did not want to be considered a fake.

He wondered whether time erases experience or underlines it: experience, mistakes, desires, impressions – the ingredients of a palatable or an indigestible life, depending on the arrangement. We ought to reject arrangement, thought Max, not wait for the abstract to make figurative sense.

On Sunday the City was –
Empty.

One or two cars, a sunbaked cathedral like an old piece of pottery in some Byzantine town just waiting to crack or be reversed into, the gathering of crisp and dirty newspapers against traffic island railings. The heat continued, stronger than ever, and the river glided slowly by, a glacier of diamonds.

Rather too nonchalantly for the severity of the occasion,

Max leant against the side of his car in the early morning heat. He was parked down a cool alley between a clearing house and an Australasian bank. Directly ahead he could see the Pacman Software building, and behind the bulk of that was nothing but blue sky.

He felt like an advert for a course in decision-making; one hand resting on the passenger door of his car and the other holding a remote-control detonator unit. He was wearing a blue and white striped shirt, cement-coloured linen trousers and a pair of Italian shoes. His fringe flicked elegantly over his dark glasses. During his campaign of violence he had got quite a tan.

Pacman hummed in the early morning stillness, its many floors and windows letting out a single tone into the heat. Max strained to listen for any activity in the neighbourhood – there was none.

Except,

the Four Tommies.

They were loitering inquisitively on the corner by the Bank of Tunisia, looking over at Max with their thumbs pushed into their green webbing belts and their toecaps glinting in the sun.

'I say, you blokes,' said one of them, 'he looks like a likely customer . . . '

Max assumed his friendly yet paternal persona, the ghost of Leslie Howard possessing him.

'Morning, you chaps!' he called out cheerfully to them 'Taking in a few of the historic sites of the old City whilst you're on leave, I'll be bound. Well, there's plenty to see, and all of it's got a tale to tell, straight off the pages of English history.'

The Tommies wandered politely over, the one who had spoken looking around to the others for their support in his trusting this gentleman as a bloke who didn't mind a chat.

'It's like this, sir, see. Me and my mates here – that's Alf and Georgie, and the big ugly bastard (laughter) at the back, that's Bill – we all thought we'd see a bit of old Blighty but now we're blowed if we can find our way back to Paddington. If we're not back by noon the CO's going to have our guts for garters and no mistake. Slept last night on a bench by the river but we was all a bit the worse for wear, you might say . . . '

Max laughed approvingly. 'Well, you chaps have certainly picked a hot morning for sight-seeing, but if Rommel's men are sweating in the desert there's a thing or two we could show them on a fine English day like this!'

The City towered over Max. He was standing alone in the street, his eyes dull and his face drawn, shoulder-blades fluttering like summer-blown petals and his mind picking thoughts as a maniac picks bluebells with a monkey wrench. Thousands of miles of telecommunication systems surrounded him, yet still he couldn't make himself clear.

He gave each of the Tommies a cold bottle of beer and had one himself. 'Yes,' he said, with respectful warmth, 'there's a quality in England that will always shine, no matter what dirty tricks Johnny Banker may stoop to. Be you commoner or earl, rich or poor, Mrs Simpson or petrol pump attendant, there's always a place in England to do your bit. To be a part of our . . . heritage, and traditions, a continuation of Arthur, Shakespeare and the song of the Sweet Swan of Avon. Let it never be said – and here Max rammed his thumb down on the detonator button – that an Englishman refused his country the very best that he has to offer.'

Max's last words were drowned by the sound of forty leech-bombs simultaneously exploding. The Tommies evaporated into the heat haze and everything went into slow motion as Max turned his face from the slipstream of the blast.

A cacophony of shattering glass laced with strident alarm bells, the screech of rupturing water pipes and the muffled thud of collapsing walls and flexible partitions. A sheet of fire swept quickly down the carpet in the foyer and behind the blistering paintwork on the window frames a roar announced the lift shafts alight.

Two years of basic designing and hundreds of man-hours of planning negotiations were put out of service in a quarter of an hour.

Max began to ramble, waving his detonator over his head like a pageant flag. 'Saw the lone Lancaster, radioed for help, saw a boat adrift, down there in the cove, near the rocks . . . a waved headscarf in the terrible storm that night, and all stations to London Bridge, to Godless January, the eye of the architect . . . '.

Sirens moaned and cars screamed into the City. Coming to with a nervous jolt, Max got quickly into his car and dodged the police cordon by minutes. He drove out of

London towards New Manderley and the sea. He had spared *Designate* at least – let them be grateful for that.

Within the hour Malcolm Houston had left another message on the de Winter Associates ansafone. 'Given the recent and not altogether unexpected destruction of de Winter's tallest building, would it be possible for *Designate* to stage the West One Fashion Week Show on a catwalk across the rubble?' He'd be grateful if someone could get back to him on that one.

3

'Broken Lute Strings and Pet Monkeys'

One: Top Man of Nothing

Summer was drawing to a close, the heat of August nearly spent. There was a chill in the clear mornings, and at noon a pale sun gilded the tops of the trees as their fluttering leaves were tossed in the quickening wind. Dusk was a cusp of moonlight traced with cider gold. Max knew that he would not survive the winter.

In London the squares of Bloomsbury – Gordon, Russell and Bedford – were three dusty pitches overhung with powdering foliage, and beyond the Euston Road, in Regent's Park, the sunshine spread moodily up the broad garden walks to convert into a rolling wilderness of bleached grass. The shabby white houses tumbled down their mysterious suburban escarpments on the foothills of north London, and down by the side of the dark canal a few of the furthest-tumbling of these stood silently in the afternoon shadows. Time stood still in this basin, the dregs of summer gathered in the bottom of a shallow garden urn. Max de Winter sat on the bottom step of summer and saw only the sea for a winter, the breakers off the beach at New Manderley perhaps, as his button hole converted to a foppish technicolour and he mused on matters of Life and Death. He had maybe a fortnight in which to conclude his career.

He felt tired, and incapable of the effort required to reason. This lassitude was complicit with the concluding moves of his mission; he had only to destroy two more buildings and then wait for the floodtide of the loosened Thames that flowed past his targets to rise up and sweep him away on a blast-severed security door, then to spiral delicate circles into the waterlogged meadows of Surrey. He would finally find himself out to sea, a crashed fighter pilot drowning in sight of his native England.

Let us consider the garden at New Manderley. In the morning, the heavy dew of late August made the grass a carpet of sparkling water; by lunch time the heat of the sun was barely enough to evaporate it. The borders were overgrown, and the thick furred stems of the larger plants had grown coarse and brittle during the summer that had burnt their sap away. The last few petals on the roses hung bronze and rusty over their darkly folded underleaves. The sky stayed cloudless from mid-morning to tea time, but in the very early morning and the late afternoon an aromatic mist hung loosely in the sparse pine trees at the edge of the cliffs. All day long the air smelt of woodsmoke and dried wallflowers. The cracks in the garden paths were dry river beds brushed with a crimson dust. The Judas-tree cast a long shadow, and at the very tip of this long shadow sat Max de Winter on an old garden chair. He brooded on his life whilst the garden bled to death.

He knew that he had treated Rebecca badly. His moods had hung around on the street corners of her life, sometimes smiling and trying to look handsome, at other times peevish and nasty, a hint of a threat in their presence. Whilst never losing sight of her beauty, Max de Winter had sat in the swivel chair of confusion with his elbows firmly planted on the desk of paradox whilst he contemplated her personality. He adored her, his adoration becoming all the more inarticulate as he realised the slenderness of the vocabulary they had in common. Their Greater Game was as devoid of team spirit as it was of prizes.

And so finally, on September the fourth, Max knew that it was time to leave the darkening garden. In London his fists would whiten in the darkness of shop doorways, all the flowers that he might bring up with him from the country would turn to tinder, and eventually, in the blast, an asphalt perfume would rise to wrap up the finale of his blighted marriage and pass it on into the indiscriminate care of history.

The Museum of Corporate Finance stood low beside the river, three pyramidal roofs of lead-welded glass under which a variety of museum precincts housed a permanent collection of exhibits related to the history of banking. These were annotated by a succession of temporary displays that depicted methods, dramas, and follies from the world of financial record keeping – the freak shows of data processing. There were flow diagrams, touch-operated displays, a talking bank manager courtesy of Tussauds, and a hand that gave out money in real bank notes at the precise speeds it would take various graduations of income earners to receive it. Part of the interest of the latter lay in the detailed description of the security measures taken to display it. Children gaped and fathers nodded with stern approval; it was after all, real money.

Max de Winter stood alone in the foyer, looking at the postcards of historic invoices, oven gloves depicting legendary account numbers and washable kitchen charts with basic accounting practices printed on them. It was a successful museum, horrid too, with its gift shop and no-smoking restaurant, its lecture rooms and crêche. The light filtered down in tropical pools, the great moments of financial history mottled by tiny spotlights.

Max de Winter's recent annexe to the museum, the Historic Invoices Library, still smelt of plaster and paint. It was a white space with ladderax shelving, a more lucid environment for the serious student of the balance sheet to extend his scholarship within.

Above all Max knew that he must not stop now, must not be dragged screaming into debate with anyone about what exactly he was doing with all these carloads of explosives and highly peculiar dreams. A sunny autumn day closed in around the last English architect, Max de Winter, and at 5 p.m. precisely the museum would close for the day. In possession of an intimate knowledge of the building, Max sneaked down one of the administrative offices corridors and hid in a photo-copying room. On the wall there was a witty cartoon clipped from the *Guardian* about photocopiers. He locked the door from the inside.

Soon he heard the air conditioning groan to a halt, and then the lights were turned off. A few footsteps, some resigned and forlorn 'goodnights', then silence.

The Museum of Corporate Finance was his.

He sat on a box of Infotech paper and closed his eyes. His father had been a wing commander, his mother a keen gardener.

All around him the gathered invoices cried out their spectral balances due. From Pooby Trust Ltd 1926 to the bill for Concorde's cockpit, the history of purchase in its documented form was represented in various styles: the illuminated manuscript of the demand, the delicacy of serrated edges where bills are torn off the invoice pad. A higher choir of fiscal chanting filled the air with its muted Miserere. The light was failing, the skylights turning blue, and a single star played overhead by the moon. From Basingstoke to Birmingham, from New Cross Gate to New Manderley the invoices fluttered like angels in the young dusk.

Max rested his head against the thin partition wall and closed his eyes. Rebecca had been using Grapefruit and Seagrass washing granules whilst he was drawing up the final plans for the Historic Invoices Library. The relationship between love and creative inspiration had always struck Max as being a stormy one. He had been well paid for his work, however, a Nation of Shopkeepers – disgusting.

He pondered the uselessness of all financial systems,

his memories diverting to the time that Rebecca had climbed up the stairs to their London flat one hot afternoon years ago with a box of houseplants in her arms.

You have to bash out sense, hack it from chaos, that's the trick – but even then . . . To build is to demolish chaos, therefore to demolish buildings is – thoughtful chaos? Who cares anyway, thought Max.

For Max, surrounded by the paper tombstones of Transactions Past, there was the sense that he was watching, or thinking, an elderly public information film, from maybe 1947. As he wondered why it looked as though the ceiling of his photocopier room was made entirely out of heavily starched aertex blouses, he could almost hear an urgent fanfare announcing 'The Voyage of an Invoice'.

The voyage of an invoice through the mind of an employee, a budget director from Crawley or somewhere with Burridge Plan (1949) housing estates – an old church steeple and a pub with roses about its door and a wishing well just outside the butcher's.

Max thought, 'I think I'm getting a stomach upset . . . ' There was Rebecca, having tea in Heal's, her gentle hands pouring out and stirring, a scone, and jam, and cream – the little laugh of self-reproach. That she might put on weight – Oh sylph, Oh love, Oh Rebecca!

And now I must blow up this monument to economic appetite, thought Max, drop a depth charge into the stomach of London's only public financial archive. Would a budget director from Crawley think twice about a mislaid file? Yes. Would history mourn the prejudiced termination of the Historic Invoice Library? What priests defend this shrine? What eunuchs of the digital watch a thin wrist, brown-suited and photochromatically bespectacled, would leap to defend this sacred place, this ardour of PR, the power behind the drone?

The invoice would appear – like writing and summer – out of nowhere, whizzed from a pre-process womb on to the stage of a freshly cleared desk. Touched down in the in-tray, it would want only out, a desperate document tattooed like a Messerschmidt or Spitfire with a number and a legend, waiting to scramble to its doom, to its encoding with PAID and the date, to when it simply wouldn't mean anything any more – when it was PAID IN FULL and dated, its demand met and its power defused, it dead (and dated), en route from the file to the dear old shredder, without any due rights or solemnity but just a number, a justification for its originator to retire to Surrey and have a beech hedge and a white gate with children swinging upon it and a rather exceptional buddleia . . .

Ought Max to light a candle in his local Collegiate Church for the unknown invoice, strewing a petal or two onto the ancient slate? It would be a pathos pact for the invoice that died for its country – that country being a queer place, a long way from Max's exotic England.

In London the meetings never end; the curiously stylised self-importance that patinas the fundamental banality of their careerist participants must be endlessly serviced by ritual, an egomania masquerading as the exchange of information. At de Winter Associates, at Rebecca de Winter

Fine Art, at *Designate* where Arabella is endlessly under-lining things, like she did at school, at college and in bed.

And speaking of underlining things, as Max underlined his brilliant career by marrying Rebecca and therefore bringing attention to his brilliance by liaising it with beauty, let us follow Max through his office opiates and paper-scented reverie to the Bloodye Battles and Historye of one piece of paper he is about to blow up.

Once upon a time there was a photocopier, and above the photocopier was a sign that said 'Photocopier'. Beneath this sign was another sign that said 'DO NOT OVEREXPOSE THE DRUM' and this written sign was generally accompanied *sotto voce* by the advice 'Never, ever, whatever you do, look directly into the light source'. It is very bad luck to look directly into the light source, and office superstition amongst the lower clerical grades sti-pulates in no uncertain terms just what tragedy can befall a member of staff who tries to *witness with his own eyes* the process of copying. And, therefore, great magicians, and budget directors, sighing to themselves as they pass by, whisper *Beware of Magic* to the curious or just plain lazy who will not put the cover down before making a copy.

The photocopier stood in an old palace that had been renovated in the middle of the nineteenth century to house the original Self & Assurance company. By 1984 the photocopier was a disgrace, being both overused – as it was – and abused – as it never should have been. The touch-sensitive buttons had long since ceased to activate the copy functions that their user symbols denoted, and the Interrupt Copy button, for instance, now released the

paper feeder. The Copies Made counter ran, blasphe-
mously, backwards, and the Cancel button made fifty
copies without stopping. The right forward castor was
missing – possibly stolen – and the paper cabinet beneath
the copy unit itself was locked for good. Someone, some
highwayman or terrorist, had had a go at the paper cabinet
door lock with a wrench and missed. A dent recorded this
deed.

At the other end of the corridor to where the photocopier stood there was a door. The door was always firmly
closed. Mr Read, to whom the door belonged during
office hours, had been frequently heard to say: 'And
remember, Joan (Bill, Jonathan, Helen, Marjorie, Peter),
my door is always open – even when it's closed.'

Members of staff frequently repeated this bit of news to
one another, their features widening with mirth as they
marvelled at its self-contradiction.

'How can a door be open – even when it's closed?' they
said to one another. They attributed the paradoxical quali-
ties of the statement to whatever facet of Mr Read's
personality they had decided to dislike, regardless of
whether or not they believed their diagnosis to be true.

Mr Read sat on the other side of the door, his head bent
over a large green file with 'Budget Accounts' written on it
in felt-tip. The file never changed, it was always 'Budget
Accounts'. At about three o'clock most afternoons Mr Read
would walk the length of his little office and consult the
Sasco Year Planner. He looked at the number of the year,
the month and the day with a smug, proprietorial look.
Then he nodded once or twice.

Michelle, a clerk typist, sometimes had to make fifty copies of a 'document' for Derek Fish, Assistant Director Accounts Department, who worked at the other end of the corridor. She would go to the photocopier and lay the original down upon the correction-fluid-scarred surface of the glass, and then put the cover into the down position, prior to copying.

On one occasion she was wearing metallic purple nail varnish as she made her copies. She had done her nails on a Saturday evening, because she was going out, and it was Monday when she made her copies for Mr Fish. On Saturday night, at Roscoe's in Essex, under ultra-violet lights, her nails had looked white. Her friend Sally had screamed when she saw them whilst they were dancing.

'Why are your nails white, Michelle?' she had asked above the sampler drumbeats and deadpan vocals.

'Because I painted them purple,' Michelle had replied. And they continued dancing.

Later on, holding her cocktail in the warm crimson light of Roscoe's Dive, Michelle had noticed with satisfaction that her nails now appeared the electric purple she had wanted them to be.

'Look Sally,' she said, 'my nails aren't white.'

'What's the colour called?' asked Sally.

'Seventh Heaven,' replied Michelle.

Having put the cover down on the photocopier, Michelle then pressed the Cancel button in order to make the fifty copies more quickly. She tried to walk the entire length of the corridor and back before the copies were made.

She spread her hands out in front of her, palms down. She looked at her chipped, purple nails.

'Not the sixth and not the eighth,' she thought. 'The Seventh.'

Heaven.

Mr Fish sat behind his desk and waited for the document to be returned to him with its copies. He was thinking about Michelle. Could an eighteen-year-old like Michelle with a boyfriend at university possibly find him attractive? It was pathetic how lovely he found her. Although on the short side, she had firm legs. He liked the black ski-pants she wore. He liked the black polo-neck tops she wore. He wondered how they made them these days to pull down so tightly over the bust. Maybe . . . it was a leotard! and he sighed.

'It must be so soft,' he thought, with a mounting sadness. He did not know what exactly must be so soft. It didn't matter. Michelle, her ski-pants, her black polo-neck top, the fabric of these garments, her lips, her body, everything – must be so soft. His eyes watered slightly. He felt comforted by the presence of an emotion. He knew that he wasn't all bad. He knew that he would never take Michelle out, although sometimes at lunch time he would walk past the little Greek restaurant in Farringdon that he had always imagined would be a suitable rendezvous.

He would be forty-eight in July. His daughter left home the previous September. In two years time she would be a classicist. The library at her university was made entirely out of glass and contained over four million items includ-

97

ing microfilms and fiches. It also contained the Harding Collection of Illuminated Manuscripts. It was a good university and a fine library. June, his daughter, was happy there.

The previous week, on the Wednesday evening, June had driven from the campus to the town where Phil, her boyfriend, lived. He lived in a house with some people. They had meals.

June parked her Ford Escort outside Phil's house. It was the first week of the summer term and everyone was talking about their exams. Phil came out of the house, pulling on his leather jacket. After June had kissed him they drove into the centre of town to meet their friends Bob and Rob and Cosmo and Mitch for a drink.

The clouds were purple over Leicester (the town). The centre of Leicester was orange; the white taller buildings a cupric shade of red. The friends went to the Marquis of Grimsby, or 'The Grim', a pub.

They talked about work and jobs and travel, the latter being something they had all done a little of but would like to do much more of. One would extol the exotica of Peru, another the need to do Europe in one go, on a train. They made an excitable and implausible plan to all go to Spain together for the summer because Spain is so cheap once you've got there.

Mitch wondered whether Jan would finally ditch Phil and pay him some attention if they ever all went to Spain. Mitch had a Greek restaurant too. Two phone calls unreturned last vacation, later ascribed to an abundance of weddings. He readily forgave her. He could never hold on beyond the point in his fantasy when she stood in front of the television set.

June and Phil had decided not to sleep together during exams. They talked a lot, marvelling at the way that sometimes things don't work out, which is strange, and sad, but usually for the best.

June Fish's father sat in his office and tried not to look up when Michelle came in with the document and its copies. She didn't say anything either and put the copies on the front of his desk and placed the top copy on top of them. She was neither friendly nor impolite, having no need to be either. Despite himself, Mr Fish looked at her bottom as she left the room. On his tiled windowsill a spider plant dangled brown leaves into a saucer of dust and cracked mud.

He looked at the document, a standard letter format for Mortgage Enquiries. It was drafted for people who were improving the value of their property. The letterhead read: 'Self & Assurance Estd. 1867.' The address followed: 'Investment House, 58-62 Bishopsgate, London.' He closed his eyes. After twelve years he still could not remember the post-code. This was a nuisance when people rang up and he had to give them the address.

'And the post-code?' they would ask, despite his hoping that they wouldn't. And then he would have to lean over awkwardly to look at the piece of headed note paper he kept especially for when people rang up and asked him the post-code.

He was pleased with the pile of standard-letter copies

that the blessed Michelle had put on his desk. They were all ready for Internal Circulation to Heads of Sections prior to the monthly Financial Systems Meeting at which their contents would be discussed and he would be acknowledged as their author.

It was a quiet afternoon. Typewriters tapped and beeped in the distance. A window was opened and a blind lowered; soon it would be summer.

Mr Fish picked up the telephone receiver and dialled Mr Read's extension. He heard the phone ringing down the corridor. He knew that Mr Read would be in because his door was closed.

'Hello. Mr Read's extension.'

'Oh. Is he there please?'

'I'll just get him.'

Mr Fish was now worried in case he was disturbing Mr Read. 'Hello, Richard Read here.' (That gruff yet approachable voice, always ready for new ideas if not new activity, always keen to sound out new blood. A lot of new blood had been sounded out in the twelve years that Mr Fish had been ringing Mr Read.)

'Oh, hello Richard, Derek here. I thought you might like to look over the letter for the Finance Meeting. I've just received the copies.'

'Oh, good. Bring them down.'

Mr Fish was pleased. Being in Mr Read's office meant not actually having to do any work, or rather it was the most work (in visible terms) that one could be seen to be doing.

He put down the phone. He looked at the top copy and

read it through. He thought about a racing bicycle with Michelle on it. The last line said 'Yours sincerenely'.

The sky was brilliant blue above the buildings across the street.

The lights were going out all over Bishopsgate. Mr Read sat behind his technically open door and read computer print-outs. He wanted to lose himself in his work as one might lose oneself in Hampton Court maze, finding pleasure in the struggle to escape. He also wanted to be free of desires, and regrets and memories. He wanted to have only the least demanding of ambitions. He wished that he wasn't alone, and was troubled by the remembrance of things that were made visible to him during his brief brushes with romance – gorse, for instance, and a particular flying club in Kent where it was always September even in March.

The old Self & Assurance building was falling down, and Mr Read found it difficult to come into the office with a sense of pride. Working late on winter evenings he had heard slates falling off the roof, and rumour had it that the west wing of the building had been known to attack birds. The ceilings were riddled with damp and asbestos, the lift shaft leaked. The gentlemen's toilet was more or less open to the elements.

He had often wondered what colour the carpets were.

But if only he could lose himself in his work! Simple, blissful routine . . . Beneath his executive exterior Mr Read was susceptible to the slightest emotional shock.

Little things left permanent scars and at night the light on his radio alarm clock seemed to wink at him mockingly whilst adverts for soap and certain late-night chat shows made him cry. It was surprising that he was the director of a firm, given his emotional instability, his complete and utter inability to communicate with people and his increasing fondness for drink. Success, however, is largely a matter of appearances, and Mr Read did look like a director.

Whilst he talked to himself in a sing-song whisper, Michelle listened to her friend Christine talking about the distraction being currently thrown in the path of her engagement to be married soon by a friend of a friend of hers who is now 'arty'. Christine had been proud of her boyfriend Kevin until she met Sean, and now there is something glamorous about the ragged state of Sean's black jeans that makes her say to Michelle: 'It's people like Sean who sort of shape the way that people like Kevin think.'

Kevin had been working hard at his business studies diploma for nearly fourteen months; he could not, however, paint, and his trousers were in a banal and conventional state of repair. For Christine there is something, some glorious, clandestine, passionate something about the way Sean says 'Really?' Also there is something mysterious and sexy about a person who can talk to a famous art critic about how long they've been looking at lines and how interesting they find them.

Kathy was working for the Self & Assurance as a Super-

Sec Temp with w/pr, s/h and skills. She saw the advert for the job in *Working Girl* magazine on 20 September 198-, an orange, blustery day, during the cleaning of the north side of St Paul's. She had always known that she wanted to be a super audio sec, possibly legal, with w/pr, s/h and skills, even as a child, and when she read about the great office and terrific perks she knew in her heart of hearts that ere the sun had set over West One again she would have convinced the personnel department that she could cope with a busy director and have a sense of humour – even under pressure.

It was her mistake, but she would never admit it.

All that Michelle is interested in is finding her seventh heaven; neither the sixth nor the eighth will do – it has to be the seventh.

Mr Read looked through his old diary. He noticed that on 25 June of the previous fiscal he had made a note to kill himself. He went over to the Sasco Year Planner and looked at it carefully before saying 'Drat' very quietly.

Max de Winter Associates were commissioned in September 198-, to design the new Self & Assurance headquarters. The shareholders were pleased, the board was pleased, and the staff were pleased.

Mr Fish sat at his desk in his shirt-sleeves, a broad oblong of yellow sunlight turning mandarin across his back. He thought about Michelle wearing a pair of blue jeans and a black bra, cupping his leathery face in her soft brown hands. There were tears in his eyes.

June Fish sat at her little desk in front of the window in

Room 6 of Merksham Hall of Residence. She had a cup of tea in a white mug with part of the *Times* crossword printed upon it. The only word filled in on the design was 'coffee'.

Her brown hair fell lifelessly across her face. She placed the longest strand behind her ear and then reapplied herself to a translation:

'Utinam populus Romanus unam cervicem haberet.'

It is Suetonius, *The Life of Caligula*. In her conscientious blue-biro handwriting she wrote:

'Would that the Roman People had but one neck.

And then she underlined it in red, because it was the answer to the question.

Max de Winter underlined the Museum of Corporate Finance by lacing it with sixteen gallons of petrol and dropping a match. Not one single invoice remained, just a few scraps of greasy black paper that settled like snow on the river.

The Voyage of the Invoice ended as ash in the Thames, and Max could not help but feel convinced that nobody would miss the offices through which the invoice had sailed that much.

He exploded myths. There were no hanging baskets on the platforms of Max's last stop. There were no dates in his diary either, just a few old photographs that became more and more of a body-temperature problem. The life of an open book.

To disown a life, to break it first, then go.

Two: Max de Winter's Apostasy

'BECAUSE WE'RE LIVING IN A MATERIAL WORLD'

In Margate there were elderly advertisements fading in shop windows for soft drinks and beers that no one wanted to buy any more. Summer Fizz, for instance, and Tucky, and American root beer.

Max de Winter never revisited Margate after the completion of his jazz-hacienda in its seaside suburb all those years ago. Someone once said it was beautiful. Some things are.

Malcolm Houston summoned his team to the meeting. 'It's just a brief one,' he said whilst they were taking their places.

'The November issue, "Season of myths and mellow . . . "; shopping guide, "Who has not seen thee oft amidst thy stores . . . " – no more puns; I think we can leave it this month. Features – Korean Holidays: "Seoul'd", Korea generally; men's underwear; Loose Grooves; Martin Caleman's new novel *PictureFright* and interview with Lawrence Crane: "Carry That Weight". Ah – "In and Out": this month's TV, Quiz Shows, "Do as You Would Be Done By", cable selection, Michael Caine on video choice . . . Yachting feature, everglades fashion, child pornography . . . Arabella?'

'Just a mention, Malcolm, about follow-up on de Winter.' (General laughter, lowering of eyes to table whilst smiling.) 'As you know, there's been quite a lot of letters in about our use of de Winter sites, and an awful lot of 'How-could-we-do-it-someone-might-have-been-killed-terror-ism-isn't-funny', but on the other hand the clothes were very popular . . . '

'I wonder if de Winter's done a bunk,' chimed in Gemma unprofessionally; 'I mean, it's a bit bloody funny that he hasn't been arrested or something, isn't it?'

Arabella frowned. 'I believe that there's only that church thing left now – they're hardly likely to blow that up, are they?'

'I wonder who's doing it?' said Gemma. 'And incidentally, why don't we do a feature on churches? You know, the ones to be seen in, who worships where, the ones with the celebrity vicars, that kind of thing . . . ?'

Malcolm noted down the idea in very small handwriting on his grey note pad. 'Churches,' he wrote and then '(Gemma?)'.

'Thanks Gem,' he whispered, nodding and flicked the point of his pen at her slightly by way of grateful acknow-ledgement for her input. Gemma immediately looked serious.

The meeting gradually broke up. A few people made suggestions as to the identity of the de Winter building bomber but fairly soon the attempts to be witty outweighed the educated guesses. As the team drifted back towards their offices their conversation slipstreamed back into the empty meeting room. 'I hear Dave Blax has started casting for the de Winter biopic . . . They want Terence Stamp and that girl with the hair who was in thingy . . . '

Arabella sat down at her desk and ate a handful of seeds from the Seed Shop down the street. The little white plastic bag had 'Seed Shop' printed on it in black capital letters.

Malcolm went to Basta Manica in Percy Street to have lunch with a woman from the Victoria and Albert Museum who knew of an opening in design exhibitions. He was tired of trying to stay awake for long enough to keep London's diary, and even more tired of writing about the future of tomorrow last week or whatever it was that *Designate* used as an excuse. A few months in the job had kindled his ambition to be taken seriously by his friends in Holland Park. He would go for art history or documentaries perhaps. Something solid. There were only so many plausible moves in the arguments In Defence of Ephemera and most of those were in French and largely incomprehensible. A book was a possibility. He knew that Stefan Durand were looking for books on something artistic. Wide margins, hushed chatty text with footnotes and the all-important beautiful printing. The literary equivalent of being chatted up by a well-dressed librarian with a colourful past. Maybe that's what he would do. There had never been a decent history of aftershave, for example – a pan-cultural jog down the trail of the scent, the history of the hunk from Romeo to Rambo . . . He'd maybe go to Minos and write a synopsis. He felt that back issues of *Designate* were tossed like unwanted bouquets onto the nearest grave. He wanted to contribute something serious. The future was such a lovely thing.

The Church of God the Truth (Tower Hill) was closed.

A black magnetic sign board with clip-on metal letraset announced the times of services, the hours of private consultation, and the last orders for the restaurant. Max de Winter watched the sun going down in the black glass of the front doors. He could see brakelights reflected in the windows. On the other side of the glass was a hedge of houseplants and potted moss.

Peering inside, he could see the Church of God the Truth bookshop. Large posters advertising holidays to India and curious roots were interspersed with garish depictions of the Holy Deity, who bore a striking resemblance to an elderly hairdresser or a second-division centre forward. His hands were outstretched from billowing white sleeves and he had a soft-core perm where the crown of thorns is generally supposed to be. Max wished all the faithful of this church could be sent on a one-way canalling holiday.

The church had been commissioned and paid for in cash by an American concern. Max was delighted to realise that he had blown up the receipt that survived from the transaction. But at the time it had all been conducted through property consultants in East Cheap – perfectly legal and the chance to do something sacred in teak. Laminated concrete, black glass and semiprecious metals had been the other desired materials. The money had probably been supplied by the wealthy and stupid youth of America and Europe who stood around in airports and places of historic interest looking for something to outrage their business-class parents with. Some put crazy-colour in their healthy bleached hair and others ran away to join an alternative religion. Max had no sympathy with them either – they just wanted to feel important or something. Who cares?

On Thursdays the church closed at six p.m. after evening purification. Thursday evening it would be, then – but how? The unused anniversary present of two Gucci suitcases could be utilised as bomb casing for light explosives. The rest could be simple arson. Max had not the slightest interest in doing his buildings in with a skilled technique – just as long as they were written off.

In the early hours of Thursday morning Max and Rebecca were talking on the telephone. Max was crammed between the side of his desk and a wall, cigarette ends heaped in the ashtray beside him, and Rebecca was lying on the mysteriously uncomfortable emotional fouton that she begrudgingly accepted as her mind.

'This mobile economy that goes up for young people', said Rebecca, 'seems to hinge largely upon a thinly disguised solipsistic stupidity punctuated with occasional flashes of animal cunning. They drift around expensive shops like the deranged predators that they are, picking lurid berries off the better bushes of London. They're humourless, like poems, they're sick.' Her voice was strained and breathless, her words coming in uneven bursts like the calypso beat of a hypochondriac's pulse. Her arm ached from holding the phone for so long. It was three in the morning.

'Above all', said Max, 'it's the need to be in company, to

be in a meeting, to be on the phone. I can't sleep until I've made a call but there are very few people whom I would wish to speak to. I want an ansafone that will only play back messages when I'm out . . . '

Rebecca stifled a yawn. She felt suddenly faint and drained. She thought about the windows in a modern flat in Chiswick, rain streaming down them during the night and a comforting cool smell of grass wafting peacefully into the blue bedroom that two anonymous friends were sleeping in. 'You were born too late, Max. You've chosen a life that is like the hardest building in London to find, right at the heart of a labyrinth, the labyrinth.'

'It's not that the building was hard to find, it's the roads that are so complicated . . . '

Max was talking slowly, his phrases dropping heavily into the receiver like an old carpet being repeatedly hurled into the same canal. He knew he was inarticulate, and he was ever so slightly bored with the struggle to make his words servant to his meaning. He said, 'There was an orgy of social and business intercourse that surrounded de Winter Associates and surrounded every other concept, character and corporation that we came into contact with. I contracted syphilis from all that intercourse years ago, and now I'm left here raving *in extremis* in the late 1980s. There's a skip on every corner that I pass by and they're full of either builders' junk or *objets trouvés*, depending on the postal district and my mood. Outside all the little houses and across all the waiting sites, beside dual carriageways and down dark alleys. Maybe they are the body bags of some authorised war, the collected dead of the mass gentrification of the future. Now that my war is finishing I can see the future as a city of catalogue design against a backdrop of ruins. The strange thing is that after love there are fewer funnier topics than outraged dissent. I suppose that one day the skips will be taken away and the rubbish they contain pulped into transporter wagons to be dumped on an estuary in Essex. Even the seagulls will think twice before they dip down into the dumps of Dartford to pick for bugs amongst the debris.'

He hung up. The night stretched ahead, empty. Fewer topics funnier than love . . . If Max was ever to deliver a final sermon – and there was little chance of that now – it was love that he would take as his theme, not vandalism, and he would speak with reference to those of the yellow polka dot sash whose perfect legs never caught the rough end of anything. Those with possession of a hero to cheer them up when their muscles are tired in some little night spot that caters for their sort. When strange doorways open in the life of some Donna or Diamanda – bit of a farce played out with lip gloss and shimmer cheeks, and it's not cheap but it seems so cool and desirable . . . perhaps. Love, thought Max, was a pastoral conceit, but he knew that his lawns were made of concrete and his flower-beds were of ice-rimmed anthracite. Beneath the drowsing chestnut trees of previous summers someone had poured turpentine onto the crustless sandwiches of his lonely and emotional picnic.

In front of the car park of the Church of God the Truth

there was a small acreage of wasteland. This battered oblong of stone-filled white mud, an urban field, was caramelised by the autumn sunshine and bordered on three sides by Bitterness, Anger and Loneliness. These non-fluid commodities were fixed by market forces, their joint effect not-negotiable within any deal of real-estate.

A petroleum slick spread its dusty violet palm across the surface of a muddied puddle next to Anger, and a platoon of adolescent nettles leant wearily against Loneliness. On Bitterness there hung a stone-scuffed notice, its message scrawled by an unknown copy writer in childish capitals, each letter painstakingly drawn out with a stick dipped in creosote:

> Our padre is an old sky pilot,
> Severely now they've clipped his wings . . .
> Good Old Padre! God for the Services!
> Row like smoke . . . !

In the past this melancholy zone had been where the Council Daughters of Bermondsey and New Cross would meet to hear the steel breeze playing through some wire. In the summer, when the dusty trees wore their blouses open, one could hear romantic lyrics like textbook Latin, the sweet voices of the girls – 'Do you, do you, do you, do you like our eyes? Our eyes are sixteen years old. Do you like them? Do you want them? Do you know about our eyes?' Ghosts.

Now, in September, this area enclosed by three strange fences contained a showroom-new Mercedes minus its windscreen and a complicated freestanding structure made out of an old ironing board and a classroom map of the political geography of the world. The coast of South America had twisted itself inelegantly around the steel strut of the legs, whilst the ripped surface of the board was covered with the sky-blue fabric that denoted the Central Atlantic. Europe, the Soviet Union and the greater part of Australasia hung heavily over the other side. There was a gash in the map between Nanking and the northern tip of Borneo into which some roguish or simply distracted passer-by had slipped a neatly folded advertisement. The capital letters on the protruding fold announced 'BREATH TA' with an unremitting confidence in their legibility.

The Mercedes belonged to Max de Winter and the loss of its windscreen to some junior vandal was of no importance to him. The sculpture – for sculpture the map and ironing board were – had been purchased by Max for many thousands that same Thursday morning from Rebecca de Winter Fine Art Ltd, Cork Street W1. He had had it placed on the little area of wasteland as a permanent loan from de Winter Associates to the City of London.

But things must mean something, however confusing their initial appearance, and translation – unseen – is difficult. There are so many attempts to be crossed out before a fair copy can be nervously handed in to history, a friend of England. The working out in the margin – that which winds up in the skip – is confusion, the by-product of translation: artificial roses dripping under artificial spring showers in a department store, modern art stacked in a builders' yard in south London – what truth value does the ambiguous product of looking for the right answer have in artistic terms? It is the Art of The Great Crossing Out, and Max de Winter's gift to the City of London was a modern masterpiece of this genre, skip-junk art and priceless rubbish.

There was a brief talk about reincarnation after Evening Purification. That particular Thursday evening found a number of the Church of God the Truth congregation sitting with little cups of fruit juice as they listened to an official of the church explain about the various stages of the Life Eternal. During the progress of the soul from one body to the next, it was dictated by the Church of God the Truth that the spirit – or 'Truth', as they called it – never in fact changed. Leslie or Janet in 1758 were the same Leslie or Janet in 1958, it was simply the body that changed. God suppressed memory at the start of each new body-tenancy and it was only to a Chosen Few, high up in the administration of the Church of God the Truth, that a kind of spiritual season ticket was made available to allow commuting at will through a succession of lives in order to return to the present and tell the faithful about God's intentions, world plan and immediate financial problems. The Church of God the Truth did terribly well out of the money raised by these teletheological sponsored walks.

The problem was one of moral purity, and the Church of God the Truth had exclusive rights to the TCP of the soul. They annexed this programme of expensive spiritual hygiene to a lot of pseudopolitical lifestyling, the backbone of which seemed to be enforced cheerfulness – the proof of which was singing, laughing and physically threatening The Uncheerful.

As Max de Winter leant quietly against a fire exting-
uisher he could not help but smile at the thought that he, a
man who had doubtless been reincarnated into his present life some twenty minutes too late and was therefore
cursed for ever with a complete awareness of his history
and that of his context, should be the chosen assassin to
blow this phoney temple of evangelical conmen half way
to the Elephant and Castle. He could only hope that those
who attended it would not be permitted the luxury of
martyrdom. They would be – it was inevitable – but he
would at least have done his bit by destroying the one
structure that associated his name with theirs, like the
banks, insurance companies and software firms that he
sought to have no relation with.

After the little talk Max left with the rest of the congregation and went to sit in his car whilst the church was locked
up. A cold wind blew through the smashed windscreen
and so he put a cassette of English poetry reading on the
in-car stereo. Betjeman's wavering voice filled the car with
a poem that Max knew by heart:

> I used to stand by intersecting lanes
> Among the silent offices, and wait,
> Choosing which bell to follow: not a peal
> For that meant somewhere active; not at St Paul's,
> For that was too well-known. I like things dim –
> Some lazy rector living in Bexhill
> Who most unwillingly on Sunday came
> To take the statutory services . . .

Soon it was time to commence the attack. He trudged through the chill air up to the main doors of the church and, shrugging, smashed the glass with a spanner and let himself in. Checking that the building was empty, he made his way back to the car and took out his detonator, coil of fuse wire and the two Gucci suitcases packed full of explosives. Like a travelling salesman crawling wearily up to the lobby of a motorway motel near Leeds, Max heaved the machinery of his vandalism into the foyer of the Church of God the Truth. He began to feel quite humorous – there was an end-of-term feeling to the exercise, the terrorist's equivalent of being allowed to bring in games.

He made his way to the congregation area where a pool of moonlight was washing around the legs of the stacked chairs. His plan was quite simple: the two suitcases contained explosives and detonators. He would connect the suitcases up to the main detonator with fuse wire and then put one at either end of the hall. Before he set them off he would douse the rest of the place with petrol.

Having placed one suitcase beneath a poster of some flamingos flying into a tropical sunset with 'Life' written underneath them in sentimental italics, he put the other one beneath the entrance to the hall. He began to wire them up, whistling 'Jerusalem' to himself in a workman-like manner. His good humour continued; as he walked stealthily backwards with the reel of fuse wire he began singing quietly to himself:

> 'I'll build a stairway to Paradise . . .
> I'm going to get there at any price . . . '

Max suddenly heard a noise behind him, the tinkling and crunching of someone walking softly over broken glass. He held his breath for a second and inwardly cursed all those he had known in the past who might possibly have a reason to rumble him. A second later he realised that retrospective threats are amongst the most pathetic of all so he abandoned himself wholeheartedly to whatever drastic measures the present moment might require. He stood up and slowly turned around. It was Rebecca. She walked slowly towards him, and even in the darkness of the church hall he could make out her face. Her eyes were fixed upon him and she had been crying. Her mouth couldn't smile but Max knew that in some posthumous kind of way she still loved him. Her hair was longer than it had been when he last saw her getting into her car on the drive at New Manderley one fine April morning earlier that year. She hadn't been smiling then either; she had simply told him that it wasn't working and driven away. That was the day that Max walked down the cliff path and threw their wedding album into the sea. Once thrown it lay open face down in the surf, and hunched upon each foaming bar in a tireless attempt to lurch back onto the shore. The soft coda of the tide had sentimentalised this blind progress, making melodrama out of rubbish.

The pages of the album had separated into two distinct hemispheres of compressed pulp beneath the laminated surface of their covers. An equatorial line of rotten stitching was all that had secured that old world to its spine, and soon the corroding ribs of brittle glue broke with the back of the book to make a final divide. As the sea flashed under the passage of a cloud the individual pages floated away, offering the loosening photographs to be christened with new meanings in the endless manoeuvres of a vast and indifferent font.

He took Rebecca in his arms, and felt her tense and nervous against him as he always had done. After a moment she relaxed, put her hands up to his face and kissed him.

'How did you know I was here?' Max asked, more out of curiosity than a fear of discovery.

'Some girl called Arabella rang me up from a magazine. She wasn't very coherent. Do you know her?'

Max shook his head. 'She's from *Designate*. They wanted to do a feature on me . . . '

Rebecca was silent. They walked over to a little stage that ran along the back wall of the hall.

'Does this go up tonight?' Rebecca asked. Max nodded.

The church was becoming darker. The fading parenthesis of detail that the moonlight had picked out was now little more than a wistful afterthought. Rebecca's road to this wired-up church had been a curious one but, having arrived, what was she to do? Who would she talk to now? What does a girl do when her hem is too high or too low, when her husband is a socially fêted architect who decides to turn to terrorism, when there is graffiti on her pedestal and a long drop to the plinth? *Designate* built pedestals out of balsa wood and Rebecca knew all about profile features and the weight they carried. If only she had been an arbitrator, or an arbitrator's wife . . .

There was little need now, in the Church of God the

Truth, for a guiding voice to lead her through the gathering darkness. 'I am not a guide,' the voice would say. The boat of Max and Rebecca de Winter's life together was now ready to push out into the night, indifferent to its course beyond the harbour wall. For them, the perfect couple, any time, any place, anywhere, astronomical navigation was simply a game of chance, with the stars strewn like diamonds across a gambler's velvet.

Max lit a sacred candle without leaving his Visa card number and brought it over to where they were sitting. Rebecca's head inclined into the little shell of light and Max recalled the rest of the poem he had been listening to:

> All silvery on frosty Sunday nights
> Were City steeples white against the Stars.
> And narrowly the chasms wound between
> Italianate counting houses – Roman Banks
> To this Church and to that. Huge office doors
> Their granite thresholds worn by weekday feet
> (Now far away in slippered ease at Penge),
> Stood locked. St Botolph this, St Mary that
> Alone stood out resplendent in the dark.

What would Society have made of this meeting? There was always someone ready to comment, some rattler in the *Tatler*, some maggot. The City slept around them. They did not know whether it was indifference that surrounded them or the massive silence of an artificial intelligence that they had become too tired, or too confused, to find stupid. Max pondered the future's assessment of his campaign of violence. Evidence would be sifted at artistic and clerical levels in an attempt to find the truth but it would never be found. There is nothing like a determination to see things clearly for bringing on a spiritual myopia. Every time a journalist passed by an accident they might think of Max de Winter, that was all. Even if Max were to step forward and remove the mask that he had worn during his disguised advance it would only reveal the plastic surgery underneath.

Across the street the vagrants were coming out of nowhere to sleep on the site in front of the church where Max de Winter's art loan to the City was standing. By the glow of a dozen arc lamps which hung from the gallows-like scaffolding in one corner it was possible to see the parcels of cardboard and dumps of plastic carrier bags being corralled about home fires of street debris. The vagrants were an army camped out on manoeuvres, a transit camp between the nothing and nowhere of London UK where the track-furrowed mud made loam lips that winter would silence with frozen water.

The vagrants quickly dismantled the sculpture, finding more practical uses for its medium of classroom map and ironing board. They harvested daily from the tidemark of rubbish that collected around the edges of the site: sherry-soaked newsprint, sex magazines and back issues of *Designate* burst out of plastic bin liners, and features on Hair Gel and Italian furniture were half read in the cold whilst Sandra or Angie, Yvonne or Bibette spread her legs to the sleet off other faded pages that flapped over all night in the wind.

The vagrants began to bed down on mattresses of cardboard, others sitting up on broken stack chairs or blue milk crates to drink in little groups around the litter fires whose lights could be seen from the Church of God the Truth two hundred metres away.

Inside the church Max and Rebecca had wired up the suitcases of explosives to the detonator. The floor was soaked with petrol. They sat side by side by the light of their candle in front of what they took to be an altar. It could have been their final marriage.

All that remained was to push down the button on the detonator. Very gently they both rested their hands upon it, united at last. The candle suddenly wavered for a moment, throwing up huge shadows and a bright light. Max turned to Rebecca and then there was darkness.

'Why – the candle's out . . . ' he said.

Rebecca softly pushed her hand down on his.

'Twas I who blew it,' she whispered. 'Dear . . . '

ORIGINAL PAPERBACK FICTION
from
FOURTH ESTATE

Martin Millar

Milk, Sulphate & Alby Starvation
£4.95

Lux the Poet
£4.95

Ruby & the Stone Age Diet
£4.95

Jeremy Clarke

Necrotrivia vs. Skull
£4.95

Frank Questing

Nobody Dick in Dreamtime
£4.95

Nick Sedgwick

Light Blue with Bulges
£4.95

HARDBACK FICTION
from
FOURTH ESTATE

Adam Zameenzad

The Thirteenth House
(winner of the David Higham Award for Best First Novel)
£10.95

My Friend Matt & Hena the Whore
£11.95

Love, Bones & Water
£11.95

David Peak

No. 4 Pickle Street
£11.95

The Cotoneaster Factor
£12.95

Jeremy Clarke

God Is Love (Get It in Writing)
£12.95

Colin Bennett

The Infantryman's Fear of Open Country
£13.95

T. J. Lustig

Doubled Up
£13.95